Books by Bill Thesken:

The Oil Eater
The Lords of Xibalba
Window

Blocking Paris

Bill Thesken

Excerpt from Genesis 2:1

On the sixth day the heavens and earth and all their host were completed.
On the seventh day God rested from all the work He had been doing, and played a round of golf with Man.

(Somehow, after the 'apple incident', the original manuscript was mysteriously torn, and the last part of that sentence was lost forever.)

PROLOGUE: 1879

The land in the hills above the sea reminded the old Captain of the Scottish Highlands that he loved and could never return to. It was cool and misty and the clouds that piled around the craggy peaks at the center of the island spilled over onto the rolling hills and shrouded them in the wee morning hours and through the better part of the day. Ghostly wafts of grey sifted through the air and he felt as much at home here since he was a young man long ago, and he went to the King of the island and struck a bargain for the land. It was not an easy bargain as the King was as crafty and cunning as the old sea captain had seen on his journeys around the world's oceans, as cunning as the cutthroats off the east coast of Africa, and the cannibals of the Southern seas. And though he tried to hide it, the King could see the love of the land in the Captain's eyes. In the end it was the ship itself that sealed the deal, and they made a pact with blood from their thumbs on parchment from the main. Each thought the other had made a fools bargain while protesting aloud that they themselves had been swindled. The Captain for his part was done with the ship, and swore never to sail again, so what good was it to him. The King marveled that anyone of sane mind would want to live on the hills that did not grow food, in the mist that chilled the body to the bone.

And so the Captain unloaded from the ship the chests full of trinkets from his trading around the

1

globe. He would trade the lot of it in return for labor from the islanders, to build his home on the hill and stock it with the food that grew so plentiful in the valleys, and shores. The ship held silks and spices and oddities, along with his personal belongings and gear, tools and clothes, and books, and kegs of malt whiskey from the old country, and in a gesture of goodwill he threw in a keg of whiskey from the homeland as a bonus to the King. The kegs he had kept secret from the natives as he was well aware of their propensity for good natured drinking of the spirits, which through no fault of their own devolved quickly into chaos. The drawback was their inability to control their savage nature when imbibing of the malt. They had a crude alcohol called Okolehau that they made from the root of the Ti plant mixed with sugar cane sap and fermented in gourds, but whiskey was something entirely different and the island dwellers' genes had not adapted to this particular brand of firewater as the Scots had over the generations. He admonished the King to drink the malt with respect for it was the food of the gods and not to be trifled with.

One sea chest alone was filled with silk scarves from India, and the islanders as isolated in the world as they were had never seen such a thing. A single brightly colored scarf would net him food for a month, and with over a thousand scarves stuffed tight in the chest, and using that trinket alone he figured he could last until he was well over a hundred and fifty years old.

The old Captain's most prized possession was his golf equipment and he kept it locked tight in a sturdy iron chest with a big pad lock on the front.

Within a few short months, using the native

workforce, he built a stone house on the promenade of the misty highlands with a view of the coastline when the clouds cleared. The walls were solid lava rock from the stream beds and the roof beams hewn from timber found high in the mountains. He filled the yards with gardens and walkways, and when that was all finished he did what any other red blooded and bored Scotsman would do. He built a golf course.

Trading his silks and shrunken heads and black onyx daggers for a small army of native labor, they cleared boulders and rocks from the high grasslands, and created long alleys for the fairways, building and leveling and smoothing the greens with sand and dirt brought from the lowlands and when that was all done he stood on the veranda of his home and surveyed the result. A nine hole golf course snaked through the highlands around his home, with the number one tee at his front door and the number nine green at the back door. He could start his round with a cup of coffee on the front porch, and end it with a shot of whiskey on the back terrace. There were five par fours, two par fives, and two par threes. One of the par threes was a nasty shot over a steep ravine, and one of the par fives, hole number nine, paralleled a cliff that fell off into the abyss, and going out of bounds on that hole was a true penalty.

On opening day, May the thirty first in the year of our Lord Eighteen Hundred and Seventy Nine the captain threw a big party at his new home, and invited the King and his entourage, and all the natives of the village to attend. There was a giant luau with roast pig and yams and sweet potatoes and every fish and crab known to man. There were speeches and proclamations and prayers to the heavens for good health for everyone and for the land, which was the only thing left from the bargain. The ship that was traded to the King had been smashed to bits on a reef not long after their swap. The natives had splurged on the whiskey, gotten drunk on the lot of it, and decided to go on a joyride with the schooner around sunset, and not used to the speed of the vessel caught a gust of wind with all the sails unfurled and went headlong into the headland. The King held no grudge against the Scottish captain, but the crew was sacrificed to the gods.

When the luau was winding down and the revelers full from the food and Ti liquor and dancing, the old captain stood before the iron chest at the head of the table and lifted his arms for quiet.

"Behold," he said in a thick Scottish brogue, and lifted out a straight stick with a brass wedge on the end with one hand, and a little orange ball with the other hand. He held the ball at arm's length over the table, and dropped it. It bounced high off the table and right back into his hand and the natives as one jumped and howled and yelled with delight.

He winked at the King who sat with his mouth gaping. "Aye lad," he said, "now that is a feathery from the old country."

A feathery was a golf ball made with cow leather and goose feathers, and when properly made could be driven with a brass faced golf club over two hundred yards. The leather was soaked until pliable and then sewn into a ball inside out with a little hole left over, and then the whole of it was pushed through the hole until it was outside in, and all the stitches were on the inside. Then the airiest of goose feathers, the downy ones close in on the body that had been soaking for days in a vat were shoved into

4

the little hole with a stick until the ball was stuffed as full as it could get. And then the ball was left to dry and harden for a month, painted with the golfer's favorite color and was ready for play.

The old Captain had a one less than a dozen of the featheries stowed in the chest, and knew that he would need to make more to last the many years ahead.

He filled a carrying bag with the golf clubs and two of the featheries and taking the King by the shoulder, made his way to the first tee, with the crowd of half naked natives following close behind.

He took a pouch full of sand that was sitting on the tee and poured out a handful so that it was like a little pinnacle, and then he carefully placed the feathery on top of the sand so that it was sitting well above the ground. The natives were all crowding around him, very interested in his every movement. They had no idea why they had been clearing and smoothing the land for the past year, but it must have some very important significance for the exertion of such manpower.

The old Captain stood tall and motioned for the natives to clear a space around and in front of him. "Clear a path," he barked and they parted before him, like the sea in front of a fast moving ship.

He took a couple of practice swings and then stood steady and silent over the feathery perched on the pinnacle of sand, took a deep breath, and swung with all his might.

The golf ball crackled high through the air and straight down the fairway; the throng of natives watching it disappear into the distance, dumbfounded to silence at what they were witnessing. And then they erupted again into jumping and shouting and cheering, while a pack of the youngest boys raced down the fairway to where the ball had stopped rolling.

The Captain smiled deep and wide, and then suddenly realizing that if the King did not hit the ball as far or farther he would lose face among his people, and so he quickly motioned back to the tables by the stone house. "More food," he shouted and he waved down the fairway for the boys to bring the feathery to him.

The King stopped them and held up his hands. "Me now," he said in nearly perfect English.

The Captain's smile faded as he handed the golf club to the King, and made a silent prayer as he did so.

The natives spread a wide swath for the King and he took a couple of practice swings just like the old Captain had, and the captain smiled wryly since he realized now that the King was the King since he was the strongest and most agile of the bunch, with the quickest mind and wit, and had been carefully watching his every move. The King stood over the ball, took a deep breath, and also swung mightily. The feathery launched through the air and landed in front of the Captain's ball and rolled a few feet past it. The natives roared with approval, and the King looked over at the Captain and smiled.

"Beginners luck," said the Captain with a frown; out driven off the first tee on his own golf course, by a savage who had never seen a golf ball in his life, bloody hell.

"Now more food," shouted the King, and he headed back to the tables with the throng of natives following him.

The party went on into the night, for when the

King proclaimed on the tee that there would be more food, more food there was indeed, and it seemed to go on forever. The Captain found out on that very night that whenever there was a big luau, the natives didn't stop eating when they were full, they stopped eating when they tired, and none seemed to get the least bit weary. Another thing they didn't seem to get weary of was re-enacting the tee shot by their King going past the Captains. And even though he couldn't very well understand their spoken word, body language was universal, and hand gestures of an object flying through the air past upturned faces, and going past another hand on the table followed by raucous laughter could only mean one thing. The Captain took it all in good graces while sullenly drinking from his cup. This was almost as bad as being back on the Scottish coast and being bested by that blasted McCormack. And he smiled, for nothing in the world could be worse than that.

Over the summer months when the days were long and dry, and the trade winds blew steady, the Captain played golf once every morning, and once every afternoon, and began to improve on his game.

Now and then he came close to paring the course, but every time an errant shot here and there would sour his round. His stash of featheries was dwindling and he'd tried with no luck to replenish his stock. The key ingredients, cow leather and goose feathers were not to be had on the island.

There were fowls a plenty, and even a sort of goose that the islanders called the Nene, but the feathers did not have the same downy texture as the Scottish variety, and there were pigs a plenty for hide, but all together the combination did not have the bounce as did the feathery made in the old ways.

He was now down to his last two featheries, and unless a trading ship showed up off shore with leather and geese very soon, his hopes of beating the course at par seemed doomed.

It was the morning when the winds were blowing from the south, hot and moist and heavy. A lingering smoke shrouded the mountain from the volcano far away. A storm was coming, that was for sure. The old Captain knew in his bones that the winds were bringing a tempest and he'd better hurry if he was to get in a round of golf before it hit.

With a feathery on the tee, and his last in his pocket he set out for his morning walk. Never had he hit the ball better; straight and true with every shot and by the end of the eighth hole he was even par. He gritted his teeth as he walked to the ninth tee and looked down the fairway that veered perilously along the cliff, and then ended at the green next to his home. The shortcut was to play the ball near the cliff so as to have a clean shot at the green, but the safe shot was to play as far away from the cliff as possible. Out of bounds there was a two stroke penalty, plus a lost ball that would be broken on the rocks far below. Twice he'd tried to play his drive near the cliff, and twice he'd lost the ball to the rocks, and never once had he pared this hole. Why he had made it so difficult eluded him, but it was as much the lay of the land as his stubborn Scottish pride that drove him to design this last hole as the ultimate test. And now as he stood on the tee with a par score in sight, it suddenly dawned on him. The winds, they were blowing from the south. The first time he had ever seen it. He could play his drive as close to the cliff as he wanted and the winds would keep it from going over the side.

"Hah," he yelled, at the fairway. "I'll 'ave me par yet, before this day is done!" And he stood over the feathery with confidence and swatted it a mighty blow, and it flew straight and true through the air down the fairway, and landed soft as a dove just a few feet from the cliff with an easy second shot to the green. The Captain half skipped down the fairway full of mirth, but as he got halfway to where the ball lay he heard a rumbling from afar, and he glanced at the mountain which was now layered with dark clouds that swirled menacing. A flicker of light traced through the blackness and the rumble came again.

"Ay, the storm is upon us!" And he hurried now. The winds blowing south all morning long were shifting from the north. His sea legs though strong and agile now from his walks along his course were no match for the quick change of the weather. The winds gusted and the feathery began to move. He let out a yell and ran towards the cliff as fast as his old legs would carry him. The feathery slowed its pace and rolled slowly to the edge and he let out a sigh as it stopped and seemed to hover on the precipice and then a gust of wind blew from the mountains and the feathery rolled over the side. He gave a shout and lunged for the ball, catching it in his left hand in mid air, a smile on his old face, but he could not stop his forward momentum, his feet scrappled on the hard surface and he began to go over the cliff himself, his smile turning quickly to a scowl. There was a thin hard tree growing on the edge of the cliff and he grasped it with his free hand. If only he would have used both hands he could have saved himself, but to some folk golf is the most important thing in life itself. His free hand could not, or would not let go of the feathery.

A young native boy was walking nearby and watched with amazement at the old man's agility as he scampered towards the cliff after the rolling little ball, and heard the old Captain yell out two short words as he plunged over the side. He looked over the edge and saw the crumpled body far below on the rocks, and then ran as fast as he could down to the village by the sea and reported the tragedy to the King.

"What were his last words?" the King asked while leaning forward.

"Oh shyte," the boy repeated.

The King listened carefully to the strange words, but did not repeat them, for they obviously meant impending doom.

The Captain's will stipulated that his land be left to all the people of the island, both kings and paupers, saints and sinners and that it was to be used primarily for golf, a refuge of the sport from the Scottish main.

A hundred and thirty years later and true to the will of the old sea Captain, the golf course remained intact. A lava rock wall lined the cliff on the ninth fairway to prevent any golfers from following the Captain's fate, and a brass plaque marked the spot where he had plunged.

To some it was the most beautiful and gracious place on the planet full of wonder and awe, while to others it was the most gruesome, tortuous, weed filled, hard panned pile of dung stretch of land in the entire universe. It just depended on who had the lower score that day.

1.

MONDAY

"It's high noon," said Bob. "What the hell?"

Harley checked his watch and clenched his fist. "Twelve o'clock on the dot. He's late again."

Josh took a last swig of beer from the can he was holding, squinted into it with one eye to make sure it was empty, then crumpled it and tossed it onto the pile of other empties in the bed of the truck, and belched long and loud then proclaimed, "He'll be here."

"Are you sure you told him noon?" asked Bob.

Josh shrugged his shoulders and popped the top off another beer. "I told him noon, take it easy."

"Next time you should tell him eleven thirty, and then he'd be on time," said Bob.

Harley looked sideways at Josh in disgust. "When's the last time you took a shower?"

Josh just shrugged and drank his new beer.

"Holy cow that's you?" shouted Bob as he backed away. "I thought it was coming from that dumpster over there."

Josh sniffed the air like a hound dog hunting for rabbits. He looked down at his clothes, and wiggled his toes in his sandals, then took off his hat and smelled the brim and nodded before nestling it back on his head.

"It's the hat," he said.

"And you just put it right back on your head," said Bob, shaking his head in dismay.

"You ain't riding in my cart," said Harley.

"Well he's not riding in mine," said Bob. "He can ride with Archie; it'll throw him off his game.

"That's dirty pool," said Josh. "But I like the way you think."

"And what about that shirt?" asked Bob. "Couldn't you find a shirt without so many holes in it?"

Josh looked down at his shirt, and sure enough it was full of holes large and small, front and back and sides.

"It's his Holy shirt," said Harley. "C'mon let's go check in so we can get in line."

"You know they won't let us sign up until everyone's here," said Bob.

"So lie."

"You know I can't lie," said Bob. "I'm Catholic."

"Of course you can lie," said Harley. "You lie every morning when you wake up and look in the mirror and tell yourself what a handsome bastard you are. Mac'll let us sign up."

"He's not working today, it's Monday."

Harley's simmering attitude turned grimmer than usual, the days were all running together and he'd forgotten it was a Monday. He was almost afraid to ask. "So who's at the front?"

"Betty. She won't let us sign up until she sees us with her own eyes."

Harley sighed a bit, but he was careful not to let the other guys hear it.

Bob continued. "Her evil, piercing eyes. Boy, she's got it out for you Harley. Or had it out for you I should say."

"Don't ever joke with her," said Harley,

"Bitch." Josh shook his head in disgust, and took another swig of his beer. "Right Harley?"

Harley didn't respond and his face didn't change; as though a piece of granite carved from the side of a grim and dark cliff was set onto his shoulders. He took out another cold beer, drank it in two gulps then crushed the can with one hand before throwing into the bed of the truck. Betty was at the front and that meant he either had to look at her, or avoid her eyes while he hit off the first tee. One way or the other his already dour look on the day just took a turn south.

Two shiny new rental cars pulled into the parking lot spelling more trouble, tourists. Out of one shiny car popped out two old farts in their sixties who looked like a pair of pumpkin eaters from the mainland, with designer pants and shirts and hats, and designer sunglasses. They unloaded their designer golf bags from the trunk, while the other car unloaded a family of five, a Mom and Dad and three gangly kids, pasty white and bored, with no golf bags.

"I'll sign us up!" said the Dad, the only cheerful one of that bunch while the kids were all silent and punching at their smart phones, while they walked behind him like bored zombies.

"Great," said Bob. "The course was wide open a few minutes ago, and now look what we'll be following."

"Being late," said Harley "is the worst trait a

man can have. Being late for golf is beyond excuse."

They heard it long before they saw it, a brand new silver Hummer roaring up the driveway leading to the course, tires screeching around the corner as it parked taking up two spaces at the far end of the lot. Archie got slowly out of the driver's seat, grimacing and shaking his head as he grabbed his clubs from the back of the giant car. "Sorry I'm late guys," he shouted to them. He was limping as he walked and eventually made his way to the group who eyed him with suspicion.

"What's with the leg?" asked Harley.

Archie winced in pain. "I don't know, tweaked it this morning coming down the stairs, it's an old skiing injury, a stinger."

"Stinger huh?"

Archie nodded. "Yeah, I can barely walk, I probably shouldn't even play, but I'll give it a try."

"So, you're injured."

"Looks like it."

"Probably from sitting on that fat wallet of yours all day," said Bob. No one laughed.

"Alright let's get this out of the way," said Harley, and he turned to Josh. "What do you got?"

Josh wrinkled his brow in anguish and shook his head in pain as he tried to remember all the aches and pains that afflicted him. "Back, neck, pinched nerves. My left arm feeling kinda tingly, I couldn't sleep last night, tossing and turning."

Harley turned to Bob. "And you?"

"Where do I start?" asked Bob. "Shoulders, knees, hands, my joints feel all swollen up with arthritis. I woke up this morning with a throbbing headache; I must have eaten something bad last night, even my hair hurts. I just hope I don't hurl on the course."

Harley shook his head in disgust. "So all you guys think you should get strokes huh?"

They nodded in unison, three bobble heads in a row.

"Well it aint gonna happen, so you all might as well just roll your battered and bruised old bones and bodies up to the tee and get ready for your daily whuppin'."

It seemed like yesterday, but it was many years ago that this tired old routine began. Friends forever, their golf game began to take on a more serious tone when they graduated from High School and got real jobs with real money. The usual quarter a hole became a dollar a hole, and that's when the game took on a new meaning. The potential of losing a piddly two dollars and a quarter for a nine hole round suddenly turned into a potential nine bucks, which might as well have been ten, and money being what it is; made the game more 'interesting'. Sometimes they just played the nine holes, but on other days they'd go around again for eighteen. The game was match play, whichever player had the least amount of strokes for each hole, won the hole, however if one tied all tied, and then the dollar carried over, and sometimes the match would come down to the last hole with twenty seven bucks on the line for some lucky bastard.

About a year ago Josh lost his job, and the bet reverted back to the original quarter a hole to accommodate his meager means, but by that time the daily match play championship had morphed beyond the money and into something akin to a mixed martial arts cage match. Even if it came down to a single quarter won, you could dance in the parking lot holding the coin high as though you were dancing on your vanquished foes corpses.

Only once had the match gone all square to a tie at the end, and they all tried to get the others to give them a 'stroke' on one of the holes if they were injured or sick which seemed to be every day, and it was amazing that any one of them could even drag themselves out of their front doors and drive to the course with the ailments that beset them.

One day long ago, Archie showed up to the course a little wobbly from the night before, his face ashen like a statue, bloodshot eyes, and shaky hands.

Freshly turned twenty one, and not yet accustomed to his newfound ability to legally drink alcohol, he'd gotten into a duel with a couple of tough guys from work and a tequila bottle. After the first hole he fainted by the outhouse, crashing headlong into the side of it while hobbling towards it, and they all ran over and worriedly splashed water on him. When he came to, they told him they would call the ambulance, but he waved them off with a pale hand. "I just need a cracker or something to sooth my stomach," he wheezed looking like death warmed over, and he half walked, half crawled to the tee box dragging his driver behind him, and without even realizing it they all felt a little bad for him since he looked so wretched, and together as a group winced as he swung the club so feeble and forlorn.

Somehow, miraculously, after eating some soda crackers Archie perked right up and won eight holes in a row and that's the last time anyone ever felt sorry for anyone else in this matchup. You could drop dead on the course in the middle of your swing, and the other guys might give you a stroke advantage on that hole, but you'd still be liable for the rest of the round and they'd pull it out of your pocket on your way to the morgue.

It was a tough bunch. Still, since Harley had been on a hot streak of late, and had taken the lot of them to the cleaners fairly regular for the better part of a month, they tried for any advantage in the book, and so getting the usual winner to give a stroke or two to the others for the next round seemed like a good way to start the day.

"No strokes," Harley affirmed and locked his truck, then headed towards the clubhouse with his gang of miscreants following close behind; able bodied men, in the middle of a workday, going off to play a game, chasing a little bouncy ball around a grass filled playground while the rest of the world strived mightily just to make ends meet. To them it was a short getaway from the realities of their worlds, a refuge in the midst of utter chaos, a moveable castle where they were the Kings of their own destiny, their golf clubs as though swords and lances used in battle to cast out the other evil and usurping Kings who would try to dethrone them. To Harley it was the highlight of his day, and he looked forward to it as a man lost at sea looks for a palm tree on the horizon. It had been a tough year, not a single smile had lit upon his face in recent memory, and even though playing golf with his pals didn't quite put a smile yet on his mug, he could manage a bit of a wry grin when he took their money.

The old Captain's stone house was long gone;

the roof torn off by hurricanes and the rock walls scavenged by Tongans to build the wall by the cliff. But the foundation was still there and the wooden clubhouse was built small and simple. Painted a dark green to blend into the surroundings, it sat up on a hill with a view looking down onto the first tee, and there was a small dark restaurant on one end of the building that most people were afraid to venture into for fear of something, or someone, jumping out at them from the shadows.

At the front near the first tee there was a tiny dusty room with equipment for sale, hats and tee shirts with the cute logo of a rooster sitting on a golf tee, rental clubs, and a cramped office with a window where the starter sat, signing up the golfers, collecting their money for the green fees and carts, and allocating the tee times like Saint Peter at the gate. An old rusty loudspeaker hung from the perch of the roof, the volume of it sufficient enough to hear miles away. Two thousand yards down on the course while teeing it up on the fifth hole you could still hear the faint metallic clinking as the microphone was being engaged and distant sounds echoing through the valleys like a babies lullaby.

"PLEASE KEEP THE CARTS OUT OF THE PARKING LOT, THANK YOU!" as you're taking your backswing. Most times, on a normal day with the trade winds blowing, and you being far out on the course, you could tune out the loudspeaker as you were hitting the ball.

Standing on the first tee within spitting distance of the loudspeaker was an entirely different matter. You were smack dab in the impact zone. The grating sound of the microphone coming to life and the amplified commands barked to those present like a drill Sergeant to new recruits at boot camp was enough to make the most seasoned veteran gnash their teeth and look for a place to hide.

Not all the starters working at the course used the loudspeaker for general instructions to the golfers, preferring instead to tell their guests in a nice quiet conversation as they paid their fees.

But Bonzai Betty was at the helm today, and rather than tell the newly arrived the local rules of the course when they were face to face at the window, she preferred to wait until they were naively teeing up their ball, happily standing over it with the soft and gentle trade winds blowing through their hair, and getting ready to swing, and then deliver the instructions with enough decibels to penetrate a nuclear bomb shelter.

Crackle. "NEXT ON THE TEE IS CRANE THREESOME. ON DECK IS CRUMPER FOURSOME. PLEASE WAIT UNTIL THE GROUP AHEAD OF YOU IS ON THE GREEN AND PUTTING BEFORE YOU TEE OFF. THIS IS FOR THE FIRST TEE ONLY. THANK YOU." Crackle.

After everyone took their fists out of their ears, and looked around to see if they could spot the fighter jet that just broke the sound barrier over their heads, the group on the tee would settle down to hit their balls and either giggle, or curse at the outcome, and then roar off in their motorized carts down the fairway to their golf balls wherever they may have landed, and then the next group would cautiously inch forward onto the tee, and if they happened to be tourists then the instructions would be barked anew.

"PLEASE WAIT UNTIL THE GROUP AHEAD OF YOU IS ON THE GREEN AND PUTTING BEFORE YOU TEE OFF, etc." Crackle.

"That sound's giving me a headache," said Archie. "Let's go down to the practice green while we wait,"

"Naw," said Josh. "If Betty doesn't see us all on the tee, she'll pass us by and announce the next guys. Besides, it's just as loud down there."

Finally the Crumper foursome was next on the tee, and being that they were about the most regular golfers of anyone who had ever played the course, Banzai Betty did not announce the rules on the loudspeaker, and came out of the starter's office for a breather.

The guys were taking practice swings and joking around, while Betty was leaning on the railing watching them.

"You can go ahead and tee off," she shouted to them, and motioned down the fairway with a wave of her hand.

Archie looked at the green in the distance, and noticing that the group ahead of them, even though standing on the green were not actually putting, and feeling a little frisky shouted back to Betty with a grin, "But they're not putting yet!" His smile quickly faded as he realized his error.

Betty was not amused. She narrowed her eyes, and the icy look on her face said clearly, "I'll get you for that someday, you bastard." And then she turned, and walked back into the office.

Harley whispered under his breath, "Man, what the heck do you think you're doing?"

"Just kidding around a little, sheesh. Why's

everyone gotta be so serious on a Monday?"

"What'd I just tell you in the parking lot? What do I tell you every time she's working? She is not the sort to kid around with."

"What's she gonna do, kick me off the course? I'm a member, she works for me."

Now, membership at the course was a whopping one hundred and fifty dollars a year, play as much or little as you wanted, and the price was set by committee to keep the course affordable for the paupers on the island. It worked out to about forty one cents a round if you played every day of the year. You could play barefoot and bareback, walk or ride, spit, curse, gamble and swear at the other guy's mother. You just couldn't bring beer on the course, and it was probably the only golf course on the entire planet Earth that wouldn't allow a single beer to be imbibed by the players. There was probably some rule in the Royal and Ancient Scottish rules of golf that strictly banned the banning of drinking beer while playing golf. The old and wise guys probably put it in there so their wives couldn't mess with their most ancient and sullen right to drink beer and play golf. Most courses actually encouraged drinking and even had little restaurants on wheels with cute barmaids delivering sandwiches and beverages to thirsty and hungry golfers, but not this course, it was all golf and nothing else. Get caught with a smuggled beer in your bag, and get banned for the month. But all in all it was probably a pretty good idea. If you considered all of the players spitting and cursing and gambling while bareback and barefoot, giving those animals the green light to drink as much beer as they wanted while playing golf would be inviting trouble. It would be anarchy, like throwing gasoline on a fire. You'd need a police escort on every hole.

Harley teed up his ball and glanced sideways at the others. "The usual?" he asked, and watched them all carefully for a reply. It was a common courtesy, though not taken lightly. You never, ever assumed anything when you teed it up on the course. You didn't want to see the other guy shank it into the woods on the first tee, and then proclaim loudly that he was glad he wasn't betting that day.

They all nodded and yelped agreement and Harley made certain that they did, and he settled in, checked his grip, and let her rip down the middle. While the ball was still high in flight he bent down and picked up his tee, not bothering to watch it complete its journey. "Best drive I ever hit," he said.

"Is it gonna be like this all day?" Archie complained as he teed it up, went through a couple of practice swings and cracked it down the right side of the fairway and the wind whistled through his teeth as he watched it angling towards disaster. "Ahhhh...." The ball fell out of the sky and nestled into the rough just inside the white stakes and barely inbounds. He shook his head in disgust as he picked up his tee, "It was a glancing blow."

Next up was Bob, and he sauntered to the tee box full of confidence and swagger while whistling a tune. A reformed landscape technician as he liked to call himself; the many years of sculpting with shovels and hoes the gardens and yards of the fancy homes in the area had sculpted his own body into a lean mean fighting machine as he liked to say to anyone who cared to listen. There wasn't a single ounce of fat on his body even though he ate and drank like a horse.

"You know, your knuckles would probably be covered in hair if you didn't drag them on the ground while you walked," Harley commented.

Typical protocol in the midst of a gang such as this was to ignore any and all derisive comments or get pulled headlong into the abyss of indecision when precise concentration was at its utmost necessity. Get distracted from your shot and you were lost. Bob didn't disappoint and seemed oblivious to the barbs and needles; as though he was protected by a cone of silence as he teed up his ball.

If you went far back in time and put a golf club in a Neanderthal's hands and told him the little white ball on the ground was food, smash it quick before it gets away, you would have a pretty good approximation of Bob's swing. It was a fast short hacking swing, better suited for chopping down trees with a dull axe than playing golf, and he came halfway out of his shoes and backwards with the torque while hitting as much dirt as ball. "I hit the big ball first," he would joke, meaning the Earth.

Harley nicknamed him 'Digger'. "I can understand taking a divot from a par three tee, but from every par four and five tee box on the course? Divots the size of small dogs in the middle of every fairway? Dang it Digger, if this keeps up, pretty soon there won't be any dirt left on this poor old course. We're lucky you don't take divots out of the greens while putting, I guess."

But his swing was usually pretty effective; he hit low mean runners that skipped head high down the fairways avoiding the winds that did unwanted tricks with a ball's flight path. Plus he was a lefty which suited some of the more difficult holes that curved to the left.

"It's an abomination," said Archie, as Bob took another practice swing. "God created man to hit right handed."

Harley sighed with compassion. "Yes, and He created lefties to show the world that even He can make mistakes. God bless the poor, and the downtrodden, and the lefties."

Bob ignored them as best he could, using an old Indian trick of humming while locking his jawbone, blocking sound from entering his ears, and hit his usual low and dirty runner down the middle that whistled and bounced and dribbled a few yards past Harley's high and magnificent drive. "Take that," he yelled and picked up his tee with a vengeance.

Josh was up next and he slid out of his slippers and wiggled his toes gleefully into the turf and squared the clubface up against the ball on the tee.

Like a big kid who loved to go barefoot in the summer, he'd gone shoeless for so long that he cringed at the thought of ever wearing them again.

"My feet are so flat and wide, they don't even make shoes that would fit."

He had a slow and easy swing that matched his laid back attitude, and it seemed as though he were swinging in a vat of molasses, but somehow it worked, he'd bring the club back long and slow, hold it for split second at the top, then kind of lean into it as he brought the club back and through in a long arc, then flip his wrists at the bottom of his swing and hit the ball effortless smack dab on the middle of the clubface just about every time. It was a beauty to behold.

"Your swing sucks," said Harley. "If you'd pick it up a notch we could probably play twice as many rounds of golf every year."

Josh just chuckled as his ball skittered down the fairway. The four buddies jumped into the carts and drove from the first tee and down the long green fairway, the youthful exuberance of a new beginning overtaking them as though it was the first day of spring; a fresh round of golf in the making and all that those words entailed, hope filled each of their hearts, hope and longing not only for a good round, but for a great round, a round for the ages, and their thoughts as pure as the driven snow envisioning every shot of theirs going straight and true and perfect, so they could beat the living hell out the other guys, and on the last hole stand victorious and tall as the money poured into their hands from the tearful and vanquished opponents groveling for mercy at their feet.

"Are you going to hit your shot, or stare into the sky all day?" asked Harley. He was in the middle of the first fairway standing a little to the right and in front of Archie who was gazing lackluster into the clouds still dreaming of vanquishing his enemies.

"Huh?" Archie snapped out of his daydream, "I was tapping into my inner golf guru."

"Yeah? Well how about hurrying up and tapping your next shot into the bunker up there."

"Back off," warned Archie who pulled out his seven iron, and proceeded to hit a high arching shot onto the fringe of the green, and then watched quietly as Harley mishit his shot into the aforementioned bunker, the veins popping out on his forehead as he shouted obscenities. The other two in their group hit their shots onto the middle of the green and Bob was sitting in the driver's seat, just ten feet from the pin with a very makeable birdie putt.

Harley thumped his shot out of the bunker, and watched as it rolled well past the pin. The round was not starting well for him and he cursed to himself without letting the others see his anguish.

Archie lined up his fifty foot birdie putt from the fringe of the green, it was long shot to be sure, but as he liked to say 'every putt is makeable, no matter how far away'. He mentally channeled his golf guru as he hovered over the ball and envisioned in his mind's eye the ball rolling into the cup, and he pulled the putter sloooowly back to hit the putt that would make his opponents cry with agony.....and then as the putter was moving forward towards the ball....

Crackle, "JONES PARTY YOU CAN TEE OFF NOW!", boomed through the air, and echoed off the trees surrounding the green, scattering the flock of birds that were perched on the branches.

Archie's teeth chattered and his muscles twitched from the sudden grating sound, the ball skittered off the putter face, and as he looked back at the clubhouse he swore he could see Betty's vengeful smiling face at the starter's window. His ball had travelled about ten feet and he still had a forty footer left over, but this time for a measly par.

"You're still away," said Harley who himself was over twenty feet from the cup. "I warned you, don't mess with her."

Archie, still swearing under his breath as he

lined up his putt again, glanced back at the clubhouse, while in the back of his mind anticipating the crackle of the loudspeaker at the very moment his putter touched the ball, but the nerve racking sound never came and that turned out to be just as unnerving. His ball skittered to the side of the cup missing it by a foot and he cursed loudly and tapped it in for a bogey.

Harley also missed his par putt and settled for a tap in bogey. "Five's covered," he said, then turned his attention to Josh who was up next with a fifteen foot birdie putt, and he called out to him. "Nuzzle it up there Josher, nuzzle it right on up there buddy." And he paused for effect. "Just don't make it."

Slippers on the side, bare feet and toes wiggling and settling into the close cut green, face like a rock, all business, they watched as Josh hit a glancing blow and his putt had a chance, had a good chance as it rolled straight towards the cup, and he half walked half jogged forward with a slight smile on his face and at the last second the ball lipped out and hung there half an inch from going in. Three laughs and one anguished groan, and he tapped in for par.

The tension was so thick you couldn't cut it with a Samurai sword; four was covered and Bob was about to roll the rock for a three and a win on the first hole.

His partners watched in a semi circle, like buzzards waiting for lunch at a dying water hole in the Serengeti as Bob hit his putt, and they laughed and yelped as one as the ball stopped rolling one foot short of the hole.

"He hit it with his purse!" yelled Archie as Bob hung his head in shame and tapped in for his par.

"One tie, all tie, carryover!" And they headed for the second tee which luckily was hidden from the curse filled clubhouse by a thick hedge.

They all looked around for the course marshal who rode around in the red cart, and when it was apparent that he wasn't in sight they all reached into their bags and each took out a beer.

"Two fours, and two fives," said Archie as he wrote down the scores. "One tie all tie, this is a two hole carry over gentlemen," Bob was in the other cart also writing down the scores, since it was always best to have two cards to compare at the end of the round. Every now and then when the days were hot and the beers were cold, someone might conveniently forget to write down a score if they lost the hole and having a back up card was the best way to avoid a fistfight at the end of the round.

The course was playing tough. The wind was blowing out of the south east which was making some of the holes a little bit longer in length, holding the ball up and pushing it back where on most days it would be freewheeling and rolling down the fairway. The second hole, the par five, was playing straight into the blasted head wind and everyone's first shot came up well short of the hill, making the second shot a blind shot over the ridge. Harley took the cart to the top to check and make sure the group ahead of them was clear. You didn't want your second shot to come raining down on the group ahead of you like missiles from an enemy camp. That could lead to trouble. He took a quick look and saw the next group on the green far away down the fairway and he gave a quick circle of his hand over his head, the universal sign of fire away.

Josh was farthest back and hit first, his shot barely making it over the ridge and heading to the left.

"Ya pulled it Josh," he scolded himself. "Should be safe though."

The rest of the group hit their shots to the right of the fairway and over the ridge.

Josh and Harley pulled up to the ball halfway down the fairway on the left by the trees. The other group ahead of them had putted out and were safe on the next tee and the green was now clear and ready for action.

"What are you gonna hit?" asked Harley.

Josh surveyed the scene, looking at the slope of the fairway heading down towards the green. He licked his forefinger and held it over his head in the wind.

"Normally it'd be a seven iron, on a normal day. But today's a tad bit unusual with this cross wind."

He squinted and thought hard, then went to the bag and pulled out a club. "Five wood," he announced with conviction, slid out of his flip flops, lined up the shot, looked once, looked twice, and hit a beauty. It loped high through the air and hit the fairway halfway towards the green and galloped towards it bouncing and bouncing and it rolled right onto the edge of the green.

"Hippytee Hop!" he shouted with glee and put the club back. "Gee Eye Are baby, green in regulation and putting for birdie."

Harley frowned. "Lucky shot."

A cart from the group ahead of them that was just a short moment ago on the next tee was steaming up the hill towards them.

"Now what?" muttered Harley.

The skinny guy in the driver's seat was waving and yelling at them and the big guy in the passenger's seat was wearing a scowl on his face, a very big and unhappy scowl. They pulled up alongside, and the skinny guy looked annoyed and shook his head as he said. "You hit my friends' ball." The big guys name was Manini which in Hawaiian means little, but at six foot four and two eighty he was by no means small. In fact there was nothing small about him, not only was he big in size, he had a big mouth and a bigger temper.

Manini got out of the cart and surveyed the ground where Josh hit the ball.

"I thought that was my ball," said Josh.

"You thought," said Manini as he sized up the smaller Josh, like a bear sizing up a snack. "Did you look at the ball?"

"Yeah, I'm playing a Titlest one."

"I'm playing a Titlest one," said Manini. "With a big arrow on it. Did you notice the big arrow on it?"

"Well, no but the way it was sitting I just saw the…"

"Look over there dumbass," said Manini, and he pointed towards the palm tree on the edge of the fairway. "There's your ball."

Sure enough there was a little white golf ball nestled in the high grass about ten feet away.

"We were trying to get your attention," said the annoyed skinny guy. "Didn't you see us waving at you?"

Josh walked over to the ball and picked it up. Titlest one, no arrow. "Whoops," he said.

which put them in a precarious position. Josh lined up his shot and hit a beauty, a big powerful blast.

Harley was in the center of the fairway and he watched the ball sail high in the air over his head and towards the green, or so it seemed. The wind swirled and came suddenly from the west, and as he followed the ball in the air he noticed too late that it was headed to the left, and long, and directly at Manini's group who were walking off the next tee.

"Fore!" shouted Harley as the ball bounced off Manini's head and knocked him to the ground.

Josh's eyesight was bad and he couldn't see clearly past a hundred yards. "What happened?" he called out. "Why'd you yell fore?"

"Uh oh," Harley muttered. Manini was sitting on the ground rubbing the top of his head and looking dazed. Josh caught up to Harley and could now see the situation. He also muttered, "Uh oh", and meandered across the fairway towards Manini who was still sitting on the ground.

"Sorry about that," yelled Josh from a safe distance. "My friend yelled fore, I guess you didn't hear it. My bad, sorry!"

A dazed Manini continued rubbing the top of his head and was talking to himself. "I get conked on my head..., and then I hear someone yell fore. What happened?" He looked over and through a fog saw Josh a few yards away and caught the last of his sentence, heard the words 'sorry' come from his lips. "...sorry..." Marini's eyes filled with blood boiling rage, his mouth twisting in anguish, his face turning beet red. "You again!" he shouted, and jumped to his feet, grabbed a five iron from his bag and lumbered towards Josh, swinging with every step.

Lucky for Josh that Manini was as slow as he was big. He held up his hands to plead for Manini to stop, and when it became apparent that the big guy was intent on doing him harm, as the five iron narrowly missed the bottom of his chin, he decided to take action; he ducked under the club as it whistled over his head again, and ran as fast as he could, dragging his clubs with him.

If you've ever tried to run while wearing slippers over a pot filled rough surface you know what Josh was up against. It was a handicap of sorts that was not often used on the golf course against an opposing player, and Manini though slow of foot was quick of wit, smiled evilly as he saw the odds were now even. He continued his pursuit in earnest, lumbering after Josh who zig zagged around the course looking back at the approaching disaster when time and terrain allowed.

The other golfers in the two groups yelled out encouragement to the player on their side. The skinny guy and his companions prodding Manini to run faster, go left, go right, while Harley and his group shouted out opposing instructions. At one point Manini got close enough to take another swing at Josh and nicked the tip of his ear eliciting a yelp from Josh who jettisoned his slippers, put on the burners, and ran straight up the hill towards the parking lot in the distance. It was the hill that finally put the brakes on the big guy, and he began huffing and puffing, and Josh began to slowly pull ahead.

When it was brutally apparent that he was going to get away, Manini flung his golf club at the fleeing Josh, clipping him on the back of his head, but it didn't deter Josh's steady stride, and he was soon out of sight and over the hill.

Manini was bent over, hands on his knees, panting and out of breath, but somehow managed to fill his lungs enough for one last shout out to Josh. "Get off the course!" he yelled.

The other players far down the fairway from the action saw the outcome, and having wagered on the final decision, settled their bets. The skinny guy and the other two in their group each handed over a dollar bill to the other players.

"Well, that's it," said Bob as he pocketed his dollar.

"What do you mean?" asked Harley as he did the same with his dollar.

"We can't keep playing without Josh."

"What are you talking about?" said Harley. His face contorted in a scowl.

"Yeah," said Archie. "We can't keep playing without Josh."

"No more golf?" said Harley, holding out hope, still not believing they would just pick up and leave.

"Not today," said Bob, who sat in the golf cart next to Archie and they began driving up the hill towards the parking lot.

Harley was stunned, this wasn't possible, they were in the middle of a great round, with more to come; he was up by two, and he was sitting on the green with a two hole carryover, he was about to go up by three holes, and he looked over at his golf clubs and started to pull his own five iron out of the bag while sizing up the still wheezing Manini.

"Ruin our game will ya?" he muttered with revenge on his mind, and then thought better and jammed the club back into the bag. "Nobody messes with our game," he said to himself. "Nobody." And he glumly got into his cart and started up the fairway.

They met up at the parking lot under the big shady Banyan tree. Josh was holding a bit of ice on the lump on the back of his head.

"Hey!" shouted Harley, "That ice is for the beer."

Josh looked at the half melted chunk of ice in his hand and nodded, "You're right, sorry," and tossed it back into the cooler.

Bob slapped Harley on the shoulder. "Great, now we have head lice in the cooler."

Harley grabbed a can from the cooler, popped open the top and guzzled the foam. "How's the noggin Josh?"

"It's okay I guess. What'd he get me with?"

"It looked like a five iron. It was a pretty good swing, probably the best shot he hit all day."

"Well I guess we're even then," said Josh.

"Were you trying to hit him with your ball back there?" asked Harley.

"No, you saw what happened, I just hit it a little long and the wind must have caught it…"

"Well then you're not even," said Harley. "Not even close."

"What I don't understand," said Archie, "is how they let that guy get away with it, pushing everyone around every time he plays here. He's a nuisance."

Josh was trying to see the lump on the back of his head in the car's side mirror. "Have you seen how big he is? Who's gonna tell that guy to behave?"

"The worst part," said Harley "isn't the lump on

Josh's head. The worst part is we didn't get to finish our game. No quarters for the winner to howl at the moon with."

"Well, it's a good thing Manini doesn't play here as often as we do," said Archie, "we'd have to find another course."

"Easy for you to say moneybags," said Harley. "There is no other course, none that *we* can afford anyways; this is it for better or worse."

"Maybe we should go back out and finish our round," said Bob, his voice tinged with hope.

"Hell no," said Josh. "There's no way I'm going back out there. Manini's group should be on the seventh hole by now and coming around the corner."

"Okay, then maybe we should wait by the corner of the cart barn and jump the bastard when he comes in," said Bob.

"Like a bunch of fleas jumping on a bear," said Harley.

"I've had it guys," said Josh. "Let's go on up to the knoll and have a beer and call it a day, what do you say?"

"I'm over it too," said Archie, and he sighed as he grabbed his clubs and walked towards his car.

"You guys go ahead," said Harley. "I'll be right there," and he watched them pile into their cars and trucks and head up the hill. He waited until they were well out of sight up the road, and then he pulled out some tools from the back of his truck, a big wrench, screw driver, and a small socket set. "Time for a little tune up."

Manini drove a double sized Ford Bronco, black with tinted windows, lifted with giant knobby tires, and waxed to a mirror shine. The license plate read LETHAL, and he always parked by the driving range backed up to the cement wall next to the cart barn, and when he was done terrorizing the course and everyone on it, he'd finish up his day by revving the beefed up engine over the red line, and burning a little rubber to cap it off.

Harley whistled as he walked next to the hedge by the driving range, glanced around to make sure no one was watching and slid under the Bronco and went to work.

Twenty minutes later he was up on the knoll with the guys.

"What took so long?" asked Bob.

Harley frowned. "What, are you writing a book? Gimme a beer." He reached into the cooler, pulled one out that looked good and blew the ice off the top.

From their hide-out on the hill they could see the whole south shore of the island spread out before them. The knoll was a well used vantage point, a lookout used by the Hawaiians in the old days to spot war canoes from the opposing coasts and islands, and in later years by the US Army in WW2 to spot low flying enemy aircraft and submarines. And now it was used by the crew to watch over the course for their enemies, and drink beer and tell lies. They could see every fairway except for the seventh which dipped down and out of view and was blocked by tall eucalyptus trees.

"Why do we even play golf?" asked Harley wistfully as he watched the clouds go by in the sky above their heads. It was a trick question, he was setting them up, and as he watched the clouds, he watched them in the corner of his eyes for their reaction. "I mean think of it, we walk around hitting this stupid little ball with a club, trying to get it into a tiny little hole that we can't even see a quarter mile away. It's an impossible game that no one can ever really win. Sure you can make a few birdies here and there, and beat parts of the course from time to time, a hole here or a hole there. But you can never really beat the course, the whole course, and birdie every hole every time, it's kinda like a Vegas casino, eventually it always comes out on top. So I ask again, why do we even play this stupid game?"

Josh was thinking hard for an answer. It was a question he had never even considered. Why play golf? Are you kidding me he thought, why play golf? The question itself did not compute in his brain, although it seemed like he'd heard it before, probably from one of his girlfriends who was tired of him leaving them alone to go to the course, but he'd always sort of tuned the question out, pretending it was like static on the radio, and just turned the dial in his mind. Sure he'd heard that question before, and it was kind of like déjà vu in a way hearing it, we've all been here before and all that, he'd just never heard the question asked by anyone who actually *played* the game. It was an impossible question, one that couldn't be answered, probably not even by the great Einstein himself. He looked into his beer can and seeing that there was a wee bit more of the liquid on the bottom, tipped it upside down over his mouth and drank the rest of it.. Ahh... beer, now what was the question again? Oh yeah, why play golf, why play golf, he tapped his head and thought hard for any answer that he could.

And then he dipped his hand into the cooler and grabbed another cold beer to ponder the impossible question with…

"I like to hit the tar out of the ball," said Bob. "It's sitting there all peaceful and quiet on the soft green grass, all shiny and round and nice, minding its own business, not bothering anyone, and I come up slowly behind it and just clobber the hell out of it. That's my favorite part. The sound of the club hitting the ball, and then watching it fly through the air. I especially like it when it makes that KEEERRAAAAACKK sound. Now that's the best."

Archie was the next to speak up and he stood up before them like Aristotle addressing the Greek Senate, orator extraordinaire, his chiseled brow jutting out, absolutely sure of himself and all mankind. "I like it because it *is* an impossible game to win, and even though it's an impossible game, I know in my heart of hearts that someday I can win, I can beat the course, I can birdie every hole, make every putt, get on every green in regulation for the round, some day, some way I'll find the swing, get in the groove, and go where no man has gone before, it's divine intervention, sort of what drives humanity itself, striving for the stars, the impossible dream and all. It's what separates us from the animals, you know?"

Harley was frowning at him. "Your heart of hearts? What, are you a chick now?"

The hackles stood up on Archie's neck and he clenched his fist. "I heard it in a tough guy car racing movie! There was a big pile up on the last lap, and the hero was gonna have to go around the big bunch of smoke up ahead to be safe, and probably lose the race, and then the tough guy coach said over the radio that in his heart of hearts he knew the track up ahead was clear and then the hero car racer went through the smoke, and came out clean and won the race and everyone cheered. A tough guy said it."

"It's gay," said Bob.

Archie picked up a large round rock and was getting ready to smash it over Bob's head.

Josh finally nodded to himself as he made up his mind with his answer, he'd been thinking as hard as he could on it while the others talked and talked, and now he was sure of himself. "I like the beer," he said with finality. "I like playing golf and drinking beer. Hit ball, sip beer, repeat."

"Now there's an answer we can all respect," said Harley. "Simple and true. You see guys; Josh is an incarnate image of humanity in its purest form, honest, simple and true to his innermost wants and needs. For there is nothing nobler in life to this young man than to drink beer and play golf, and he is not afraid to admit it in public to his peers."

"His peers, and his beers," said Archie as he relaxed his hand on the rock and sat back down.

They all watched Harley, waiting for his answer and he sat there sullen and retrospective, thinking and thinking, and finally he pointed his finger at Archie. "I like playing golf for the mere pleasure of whupping up on you, and you, and you." And he pointed at each of them in turn, and then pointed back at Archie, holding his index finger straight at him. "But especially you."

And it was true; he loved nothing more than

beating up on Archie on the golf course. He didn't always win, but when he did, he savored it like a beam of light from heaven. It was one of the best things that life had to offer. He not only thoroughly enjoyed it, he lived for it. It seemed like all through their lives it was Archie who got all the breaks, fell backwards into piles of money, got all the nicest girls. He even had three 'holes in one' on this very course, to a big fat zero for the rest of them. He led some kind of weird charmed life. He got a dirt bike when he was ten; his parents took him to Disneyland every year when he was little, bought him a brand new car the minute he got his license. When they were in High School he was the only one in their group who didn't struggle with the horrors of acne. While the rest of them desperately scrubbed their faces with zit medicine daily in a pitiful losing battle against the social equivalent of the plague, Archie grew a cool little beard and a moustache. He was like a seventeen year old beatnik strolling across campus with a flock of girls following him around like groupies in his rock band while the rest of them hid in the shadows like lepers from the Bible. But out here on the golf course everything was equal. No amount of charm, or beatnik beard, or money in the bank could help you sink a ten foot putt for birdie when all the chips were on the line, and the competitors were all standing behind you and putting the mojo on you. Without the prospect of whupping up on Archie, life these days might be a little too unbearable.

"Gee Harley," said Josh. "That's a little harsh don't you think?"

"Yeah, I thought we were friends," said Archie.

"But of course we are," said Harley. "We're the best of friends. And that's what friends are for, to whup up on you whether it be golf, or pool, or tennis or tiddlywinks. It puts the whole world order in perspective don't you think? It wouldn't be much fun to whup up on an enemy, now would it? After all, that would be more like work than fun."

The rest of them pondered Harley's answer and silently sipped their beers while the birds in the forest around them sang and the clouds overhead slipped quietly by.

Harley had a pair of high powered binoculars and was surveying the scene down below at the golf course. He could see Manini and his group on the ninth tee. "There they are," he said, "finishing up their tainted round."

"Let me see," said Archie as he grabbed for the glasses.

"Heck," said Bob. "That guy's so huge you don't even need binoculars to spot him."

Josh was tired of the whole thing and was firing rocks at a nearby tree. "So what," he said "It's Monday, where are we going for the game?"

Monday night football was a tradition with the crew, and they usually split their action between the only two restaurant bars in town. Their reasoning behind this was economically sound, for if one of the bars went out of business due to lack of customers, the other one would surely raise their prices on their food and beers. As it was, the two bars were in a price war for business, and were always trying to one up the other with specials, live music and gimmicks.

"It's a junk game," said Harley. "Rams and the

Saints, they both suck this year."

"Lambs and the Aints," lamented Bob.

Josh fired another rock at the tree and missed. "Yeah you're right; they'll both probably try their darndest to lose the game so they come in last place and get a better pick in the draft."

"So what's it gonna be, the Pit, or the Cave?" asked Bob.

"I told Marlena I'd meet her at the Cave," said Archie.

They all looked at him with puzzled faces. Marlena was Archie's new girlfriend, although none of them had actually met her, or gotten more than a passing glimpse of her. It was almost as though Archie was keeping her as a hostage. She moved to the island a few weeks ago, and was the new ballet instructor at the local dance studio. Originally from Brazil, she was tall, tan and from all reports had the meanest figure anyone had ever seen. Every girl was instantly jealous of her and had their nails out, and every single guy on the island scampered around her feet like little puppies, pleading with her to pick them up when she first arrived, but so far she turned everyone down. In fact Archie was about the only guy on the island who hadn't hit on her, and they were all puzzled at first how he ended up with her.

"You're bringing a dame to the game?" asked Bob.

"That's like bringing a bag of chips to a luau," said Josh.

"Like bringing a bucket of balls to the driving range," said Bob.

"Like bringing an anchor to a swim meet," added Josh.

Harley frowned at Josh. "An anchor to a swim meet?"

"Yeah," said Josh, "you know; it weighs you down."

"How are we gonna curse?" asked Bob. "Tell lies, pick up chicks, harass the help, you know, just be ourselves."

"When did having a girl around ever stop you from doing that?" asked Archie. "Heck, you did all of that with your girlfriend sitting right next to you every day, until she dumped you."

"Well if you're going to bring a girl to watch a football game, it might as well be Marlena," said Josh as he high fived bumped Bob. "You know what I'm saying?"

"I've never even seen her, how would I know?" asked Bob.

"You really are a stick in the mud, aren't you?" said Josh. "Haven't you heard the reports? She's hot, right Archie?"

They all looked at Archie for his response. Sure she was hot, but would he admit it and give up any juicy details; that was the question now riding on their minds.

Archie the stoic was trying to hide a grin the size of the Grand Canyon and finally gave up. "Well guys, I've got some big news, so I might as well tell you all right now. I'm gonna ask Marlena to marry me."

Bob and Josh looked at him with blank faces, and then burst out laughing.

Archie's smile disappeared. "No, really, I am."

"Right," said Harley. "You're going to give up the good life you've built up. You've got tons of money, drink beer and play golf whenever you want to."

"Money and beer." said Josh.

"Yeah and more money," said Bob, pointing back at Josh.

"You can travel around the world, picking up women wherever you want," said Josh. "You can have a girl in every town and just travel around picking up more whenever you get tired or bored of the last one."

"I don't want any other girls," said Archie. "I'm ready to settle down, with Marlena."

Bob laughed. "Holy cow, you're serious?"

"As serious as a punch in the face," said Archie, gritting his teeth and clenching his fist.

From the parking lot below they heard the roar of an engine, a very loud engine coming to life. It was Manini's truck.

"What the hell kind of motor does he have in that beast?" asked Bob.

Harley was looking through the binoculars and he could see Manini's giant head in the truck as he gunned the engine, a big evil smile on his huge face as the engine roared, and he punched the gas pedal down and let it up, down and up, over and over, revving the engine, the rolling sound of it drowning out every other sound within a two mile radius.

"It's a four forty big block, hemi, headers, nitro, the works," said Harley. "It's built for a drag strip. It's illegal for street use, and I don't know how he gets away with driving it on the road."

Manini locked the front wheels with his hand brake, put it in gear, popped the clutch and floored the engine, he was pissed off today and the rear tires smoked as they spun and the back of the truck bucked up and down. The parking lot filled with clouds of hot black stinking rubber and the sound of the screeching tires echoed throughout the canyons and hills. There was a clearing in front of Manini through the parking lot to the road and he popped off the front brake so he could burn his rubber through the lot. Unknown to Manini, the Bronco was in reverse, and it slammed into the block wall behind it, and plowed halfway into the structure before it finally stopped, wedged tight into the concrete block wall. The airbag blew and pinned Manini into the seat as the engine froze and blew the heads off the cylinders. The black and white cloud of smoke mixture from the concrete and rubber billowed high into the air, and people came running from everywhere, and helped Manini get out of the truck. He was stunned at first and stumbled around in shock trying to catch his breath, and then he began swinging his arms in the air as he surveyed the smashed truck and garage. A piece of roof slid down onto the hood.

"Whoa," said Josh.

"Whoops," said Harley. "Looks like he had it in reverse."

The smoke from the crash began to clear and then another source of smoke appeared from the rear of the truck that was implanted in the cart barn. The gas tank had cracked and a spark from the axle ignited some gas that dripped onto the ground. Betty came running down the hill with an extinguisher and Manini grabbed it from her and sprayed the foam at the truck. A little flame appeared by the gas tank, and then became an orange geyser. The crowd ran away from the Bronco while Manini sprayed the last of the extinguisher and then threw the empty canister at the truck then turned and ran as the Bronco exploded and catapulted him in the air, and he ended upside down next to a car as debris rained down on the lot.

Archie jumped up and yelled. "Damn, what the hell!" Which was about the most anyone had ever heard him curse.

The Bronco was fully engulfed in flames, and sirens could be heard in the distance coming from the town.

Up on the knoll, the boys were all stunned, their mouths agape at the scene below, all except for Harley who was passive and wore a non expression on his face.

"So you're getting married huh?" said Harley, ignoring to the radical scene down below. "To a girl you met about two weeks ago."

Archie couldn't take his eyes off the fireball, and then the question that was asked seeped into his consciousness.

"Well, I'm going to 'ask' her to marry me," he said. "I don't know if she'll say yes. My big plan is to fly with her to Paris on Thursday night and spend Friday and Saturday touring the city, going to the museums, the Eiffel tower, lunch by the Seine, you know the usual tourist stuff, and then pop the big question over dinner at some swank restaurant overlooking the city. I've got the plane tickets all lined up, first class."

"This Thursday night?" asked Harley.

"Yeah, it's top secret though. You're the only ones I've told far so keep your mouths shut."

"Paris huh?" said Harley.

"First class, all the way. Champagne, caviar and Paris. They say it's the most romantic city in the world."

"In the springtime," said Harley.

"What?"

"The most romantic city in the world in the springtime," repeated Harley.

"What's your point?" asked Archie.

"It's November genius," said Harley. "It's currently fall, not spring."

"Minor detail,"

"I don't know," said Harley. "Could be a deal breaker, you should probably wait, give her time to get to know you."

"Wait until spring? That's next year. Not a chance pal. It's now or never. If she says yes we'll honeymoon in Paris in the springtime. I'll make it a part of the package."

"Boy, you're really in hurry aren't you?"

"She's a ballet dancer Harley."

"Your point being?"

"They don't last very long on the market."

"You're referring to your girlfriend as a product?"

"That's not what I meant."

"She's on the market, your words, and you're offering her a package deal. That makes her a product." Harley paused for effect. "And what if she says no?"

Archie smiled knowingly. "She won't, not to this." He took a deep breath and pulled a large felt covered box out of his pocket and opened it up. Sparkling up at them was the biggest diamond ring any of them had ever seen. "There's not a girl on the planet that would say no to this. I picked it up this morning."

Bob whistled. "Wow that sure is a big Zirconium."

"It's a diamond pal, three and a half carats."

"Are you sure it's a diamond? It's so dang big it looks fake."

Harley studied it from afar. "How much did that rock set you back?"

"You don't want to know."

"What, a thousand?"

Archie laughed and shook his head. "Trust me; you really don't want to know."

"Two thousand? C'mon, it can't be more than three thousand tops."

"Twenty five grand," said Archie. "It's top of the line, double cut, the guy assured me it was prime…"

"That's not an engagement ring, it's a bribe."

"It's a payoff, the 'ol payola."

Josh laughed as he looked closer at the ring. "How are you going to know she wants to marry *you*, and not the *ring*?"

"He's got a point," said Bob, "you're going about it the wrong way. You really need to know if she wants to marry you, and not the big ring, so you offer her an itsy bitsy tiny diamond first, like a test, and if she passes the test, *then* you buy her a big ring."

"Yeah, you're doing it backwards," said Josh.

Archie's face scrunched. "Are any of you guys married? Have any of you ever even come *close* to asking a girl to marry you?" They all looked away, and he finished. "Well shut the heck up then."

"What if she says yes, takes the ring, wears it around for awhile, and decides she doesn't really want to get married. Because once she gets to know you, she's gonna have second thoughts. Does she get to keep the ring? Can she sell it and pocket the cash?"

"She's not that kind of person, I can tell."

"You've known this girl for a total of around fifteen days and you're going to give her, or try to give her, a ring that costs more than what a lot of normal people make in a year."

"I'm not asking you guys for permission to marry her; I'm just telling you what I'm planning on doing. You can back me up, or back off, take your pick."

He could tell they weren't convinced.

"Look, you'll see what I mean when you meet her. I'm not letting this one get away. You'll like her, I'm telling you she's cool."

He put the ring back in his pocket held out his fist and bumped it with Harley's. "I'll see you guys at the Cave."

Archie drove off in the Hummer and they watched in silence as the silver car disappeared around a bend of the road by the ninth fairway.

"Well guys," said Harley. "There goes our golf game."

"What do you mean?" said Bob.

"You think this Marlena dame is gonna let him play golf with us whenever he wants? You're dreaming. Those days are over my friend, she'll have him handcuffed and hogtied in no time."

Josh thought for a moment and popped the top

off another beer as his face scrunched in disgust. "That bitch."

"We'll have to find another fourth."

"How do you know Marlena won't let Archie play golf with us anymore?" said Bob. You've never even met her before, none of us have."

"I know women."

"You've known just about one woman, and she's a real ball buster."

"My point exactly, all it takes is one. They'll take whatever you have, whatever good or fun you have in your life, and they'll twist it and crush it, and smash it to pieces, and you'll be left with absolutely nothing." Harley crushed his beer can into the dirt with his heel.

They hung their heads in remorse. There would be no more playing golf with Archie at the Captain's course. No more banter and camaraderie in the finest tradition of haggling over a quarter a hole. No more all expense paid trips to Las Vegas to play those pristine courses. No more hanging out at Archie's beachside house. You see, Archie was rich, and even though they fought tooth and nail over a single dollar at the Captain's course, Archie took them on golf safaris, and had big barbecues at his house for all his friends. He always had a refrigerator full of steaks and beers and mashed potatoes. They never had to worry about him getting married and taking it all away, because as he always used to tell them, 'it's just too much fun being a bachelor'. But now, somehow, like a bolt out of the blue, those days were numbered.

"Well, it was fun while it lasted guys, I guess those were our glory days," said Josh.

Bob crushed his beer can and threw it on the pile. "Yeah it was okay I guess. Let's go meet Marlena and wish them good luck."

"Don't forget that Archie said it was a surprise," said Harley.

2.

The Cave billed itself as the ultimate sports cave, a twenty first century High Definition sports cave with one foot in the Triassic era. The waitresses wore fake leopard skin leotards and bones in their hair, and there were exotics on the menu such as Brontosaurus burgers, and Pterodactyl wings. You walked in the front door and it was like you were walking into a prehistoric jungle cave with giant ferns, rock walls covered in primitive wall paintings and giant flat screen TVs with every game in HD. Jungle sounds were piped in with hidden speakers, and a light mist from dry ice hung in the corners. The flame broil pit was right in the center for everyone to see and when it really got going the crackling sound and whoosh when the fat hit the flame, the light dancing on everyone's faces and the cave walls gave the place a primordial vibe. It was like being in a real Caveman's cave.

Sometimes, after a few too many tequila shots, the patrons took it a little too far and you'd have Neanderthal man vs. Cro-Magnon battles, and that's why they had Bubba as the bouncer. He was dressed in a lion skin loin cloth, weighed over three hundred pounds and at one point in time would regularly put Manini in a head lock and make him cry. You see Bubba was Manini's big brother, and while Manini was a big mean guy, Bubba was bigger and meaner and carried a cave man club that he carved out of a tree trunk. And where Manini had an inner need to show everyone how big and mean he was, Bubba was more refined and calm, reserved even by comparison, but everyone knew not to cross him.

One night long ago, a huge Samoan from Kalihi came to the Cave hell bent on making trouble. He drank half a bottle of tequila in one gulp at the bar, let out a war cry and picked up a chair and was about to throw it through a window when he felt a hand on his arm like a vise grip.

"Please leave the chair alone," asked Bubba calmly.

The Samoan took a swing at Bubba, and Bubba conked him upside the head with the club, put him in a headlock and dragged him outside where he sat on him till the cops came. Nobody messed with Bubba.

Archie smoothed his hair back and looked at himself in the mirrored window outside the Cave.

"You look like a fresh turd," said Harley as he walked past and into the open doorway. The Cave was hopping tonight. Just about every table was full and the fire pit was flaming away. Bubba was at his usual spot by the entrance, sitting on a stool, his war club resting on his leg. He could greet you, beat you, and bounce you out the door without even getting off his chair.

Harley nodded at him. "Busy night."

"Yeah," said Bubba. "Tourist season. The snow birds are early this year; must be getting chilly back east." The colder it got on the mainland USA, the more people headed to the Islands to thaw out. "You hear what happened to Manini's truck?" asked Bubba.

"I did," said Harley. "Is he alright?"

"He's okay, but the truck is totaled, melted into a lump of metal."

"Man, what happened?"

"The dumbass tried to drag race with the tranny in reverse."

"That's a damn shame," said Harley, and he shook his head with remorse.

"Yeah, that's my brother alright. He's not the sharpest tool in the shed, and I'll put him in a headlock next time I see him, but if I ever catch anyone messing with him, I'll crush them like a bug."

Bubba clenched his fist and Harley could hear cartilage cracking.

"Yeah well," said Harley. "I don't think anyone's stupid enough to mess with Manini, or you."

"My truck's been acting up," said Bubba.

"Tranny?"

"Hell no, I don't race it, it's for getting to work."

"So what's the trouble?"

"There's a grinding noise in the front left wheel when I go around corners."

"Sounds like a bearing. Bring it by the shop and we'll take a look."

Archie came in the entrance and craned his head looking for his date.

"What's up slick?" said Bubba with a smirk.

"Bubba," said Archie. "Tough luck with Manini's truck today."

"How'd you hear about it?" asked Bubba.

"Well, we were right th…"

Harley bent down quick and slammed his elbow in Archie's' stomach. "Hey look a quarter!" he shouted, as he pretended to find money on the floor.

Archie bent over wheezing trying to catch his breath with the wind knocked out of him. Harley helped him through the entry way and ushered him away from Bubba as more patrons came through the door. "Waitress," he said. "Water please." He grabbed a cup of water from a tray as the waitress walked by heading to a table.

"Hey!" she shouted at him angrily and kept on her way.

"What the hell is wrong with you?" coughed Archie as he stumbled through the restaurant.

"Ixnay on the Manini truckay," whispered Harley into his ear as he tried to force feed Archie the glass of water and waved at Bubba. "It's all okay, under control!"

Bubba scowled and shook his head.

"Hey, there they are, over there," said Archie and he pushed Harley away. "They saved a table for us, and in a great spot."

Sitting at a round table for ten was Archie's date and future Mrs. Crumper beaming at them. With her were three of her friends who were frowning as they saw them walking towards the table. There was Marlena, Melissa from the Hotel, Angie from the airport, and Bonzai Betty. Josh and Bob had caught up and the four golfing buddies made their way through the frenzy of the Cave towards their doom. Marlena threw her arms around Archie and squeezed and kissed him as the others looked on awkwardly.

"Oh, I brought some friends," said Marlena. "I hope that's okay."

"The more the merrier!" shouted Archie over the noise of the restaurant.

Marlena gestured to the girls, "This is Melissa,

Angie, and my new best friend, Betty."

"And this," said Archie, as he motioned to his motley crew, "is Bob, Josh and Harley."

"I'm so glad to finally meet Archie's friends, I've heard so much about you all," gushed Marlena.

"Oh, I'll bet you have," said a glum Harley as he sat down opposite Betty. Probably best to keep the table in between them.

"So Harley," asked Marlene. "Is that your nickname because you ride a motorcycle, or is it your given name?"

"Given," stated Harley flatly. He put on his sunglasses to cut the glare from Betty's eyes.

"Harley's Dad was a wisecracker," said Archie. "His Dad's name was David, and he thought it would be funny to have a kid named Harley, so that when he walked down the street people would point and say, 'Look, there's Harley, David's son'."

Marlena repeated the words, "Harley, David's son, Harley, David's son." And then she laughed. "Like the motorcycle. It's a nickname, and a name. I think that's adorable."

"Just over the top," deadpanned Betty.

"Good old Dad," said Harley.

"And you Bob, work at the airport with Angie."

"I've seen her around," said Bob and tipped his forefinger towards her. "We work on opposite sides of the operation."

"And Josh, you used to work at the hotel with Melissa."

"Yeah," said Josh and motioned for the waitress, and made a sign to bring drinks, quick. "I got fired."

"For sleeping on the job," said Archie.

"More like sleeping around on the job," snorted Angie, as she and Melissa laughed.

Bob smiled and gave a fist bump to Josh and shouted, "That's right!" ending the girls cackling. Now the three girls were all glaring at the three guys while Marlene took it all in.   And it was all becoming very apparent. She scrunched her brow. "So you all know each other, like really know each other, if you know what I mean?" asked Marlena.

Archie motioned to the group.   "Bob dated Angie, Josh dated Melissa, and Harley dated Betty."

"We're all single now if that's what you mean," said Harley.

"We know each other a little too well, if *that's* what you mean," said Betty.

"Oh," said Marlena.

"You mean 'Uh Oh'," said Archie.

The waitress brought their drinks and set them down. Archie, still standing with Marlena raised his beer glass.   "A toast," he said, and they all reluctantly raised their glasses. "To old friends, and to new friends."

A mix of grumbling ensued as the group sipped their drinks. Archie frowned at their reaction and then spotted the owner of the Cave behind the bar. "Hey, c'mon, there's a friend I want you meet," and pulled Marlene towards the bar, glaring back at his pals as he went.

The table was silent as they watched them go.

"Alright, let's cut to the chase," said Harley.

"Now what?" said Betty.

"We've all got a bit of history together, right?"

"So?"

"So let's keep it that way. History, you know

past tense. Let's keep us," and he gestured to the table, "in the past, and we can all be less tense. What do you say?"

They all nodded in agreement.

"Sounds good to me!" said Josh. He got up to leave and Harley pushed him back into his seat.

"Now let's take a look at Archie and Marlena," he asked the group. "They make a good couple don't you think?" All eyes drifted to the bar.

Marlena was laughing at something Archie had said, slapping him on back.

"Sure, they look happy," said Melissa, "for now. Just give them some time…"

"Exactly," continued Angie, "give them some time to get to know each other…"

"And bam!" Bob finished her sentence for her. "Past tense."

"But what if they continue to get along?" mused Harley. "What if they continue to get along so well in fact that they decide to take the next step?" They all looked back at the bar. Now Archie was laughing at something that Marlena had said.

Harley's voice turned somber as he continued, "Archie's going to ask Marlena to marry him in Paris this weekend."

Betty was perturbed. "So what?"

"So what if she does say yes and they do get married, then we can have many, many more of these little get togethers, all of us bound as one. Their history will be our history for the rest of time, and we'll live it together, just like one big happy family."

"That bastard," seethed Angie.

"We're in," said Betty. The other girls nodded.

"What's the plan?" asked Melissa.

Harley took a sip of his beer. "There is no plan, yet."

Betty frowned. "Typical."

"Look, we just found out about it," said Josh. "And that's another thing, Archie told us in confidence, so just keep it to yourselves, don't go yapping to Marlena as soon as our backs are turned."

"Now you've gone and done it," said Bob.

"What are you talking about?" asked Josh.

"I read a research paper the other day; four out of ten women are unable to keep a secret. I would wager we have three out of those four sitting right here."

"Take a hike," said Melissa. "We can keep a secret, if we want to that is."

"The research paper also said that the average time for a woman to reveal a secret is forty seven hours and fifteen minutes."

Melissa scoffed. "The most amazing thing about your statement is that you can read."

"It was in a magazine at the dentist's office. I was bored."

"Look pal," said Betty. "It's like Melissa says, we can keep a secret, if we want to. Key words, IF we want to."

It was Harley turn to scoff. "Yeah right."

"In fact, in this case I think the best scenario is to not tell her that Archie is going to propose to her in Paris," said Betty.

"No?" said Angie.

"I think she really likes this guy," said Betty. "She might just think marrying him is a good idea."

"Eeww," said Angie.

"Yeah," said Betty. "And then we'd either lose her as a friend, or be forced to hang out with these losers all the time. We need to find a way to nip this in the bud."

Angie pointed at Bob. "Why don't you guys just stop hanging out with Archie. And we can keep Marlena. Problem solved."

"Archie's our best friend," said Bob. "We've been hanging out together since we were in kindergarten."

"Don't you think that's long enough?"

"Why don't you girls, and I use the term loosely, stop hanging out with Marlena, and then Archie can have her and we can have peace on earth."

"Don't forget about the golf," said Harley.

"Oh yeah."

"What about the golf?" asked Betty. She looked from Harley to Josh to Bob and back to Harley. A smile formed at the corners of her mouth. "Oh, I get it, you think Marlena will get in between you and your little golf game? It that what this is all about?"

"It was," said Harley. "Until we saw Marlena's friends. Now we have two reasons."

"You and your little game. Pathetic."

"You see guys," said Harley, "here before us is proof that there is a genuine hatred among women for the game of golf."

"It's not hatred," said Betty. "It's called clear reasoning, most normal people don't play golf every day."

"I think they have need issues," said Melissa.

"Yeah we do, it's called the need to play golf," said Harley to cheers from his gang.

Betty had her drink in her right hand, and was ready to launch it across the table at Harley, but Melissa had a vice grip on her wrist. "Not here," she said.

"Okay, okay," said Betty and released the glass. "How are we going to work this blockade?"

"No plan?" asked Melissa.

"We'll work out a plan and get back to you," said Harley.

Betty leaned across the table. "How about if we work out a plan and get back to you?"

"Funny."

Angie pointed at Josh. "How about we just tell Marlena what slime balls you losers are, and that her new boyfriend is a carbon copy.

"Except with more money," said Melissa.

"A lot more money," said Betty, and her gang of girls laughed.

Harley leaned on the table. "Hey listen, we've got money, I've got money."

"Oh yeah?" said Betty. "How much money you got in your wallet right now Harley?"

"Getting kind of personal, aren't you?"

"Yeah, just like I figured. You're broke."

Harley looked at his friends and shook his head. "You see guys; it's just like when we were dating. How much money do you have Harley, what's in your wallet Harley? Some things never change." He took another swig of beer and shook his head in dismay, deeply disturbed.

"Be a man for once and fess up Harley," said Betty. "You didn't bring any money to the restaurant did you? What is it this time? The check's in the mail? You left your wallet in your other pants?

Show us your wallet Harley, and this round is on me. I'll buy."

Harley was glum. He patted his pants and shook his head.

"C'mon Harley," said Josh as he grinned. "Show her. Free beer."

Bob chimed in. "Yeah Harley, get her."

"Other pants my eye," said Betty.

Harley sighed. "It's worse than that"

Betty sat knowingly back in her chair and nodded to her friends. "Here we go."

"My wallet," began Harley, "stuffed to the brim full of cash, bursting at the seams in fact with the devout purpose to buy rounds of drinks and hordouvres for all of you..." as he gestured magnanimously to the table, while the guys leaned forward anxiously, and the girls shook their heads in disgust, "is alas still in my golf bag, which I have mistakenly left back at my garage. I am currently..." he threw a hard glance at Betty, "though not absolutely... penniless."

"You're penniless as far as these beers are concerned," said Betty to cackling.

"I was counting on you," said Bob. "I left my wallet on the counter at home."

"I don't even have a wallet," said Josh. "I just figured Archie would cover us like he always does, and I left my big bag of money at home."

"You're a pig," said Melissa.

"Hag," countered Josh.

They all sat silent trying to avoid each other's eyes while sipping on their drinks.

"Well isn't this nice," said Archie as he and Marlena came back to the table.

"I love Monday night football," said Marlena, beaming like a ray of sunshine on a stormy day.

Archie pointed to the drinks and motioned for the waitress to bring another round. "Now tonight is all on me guys and girls, no arguments, my treat. And next week I want to host a little party for everyone, I might have some very big news to announce." He winked at Harley.

"Yay," said Betty forcing a smile.

"One big happy family," said Harley through clenched teeth.

Later on, after they'd eaten their meals and when Archie and Marlena had gone back to the dance floor, they huddled in conspiracy over the table.

"Alright," said Harley, "I've got an idea, we'll spread a little innuendo about our two little love birds."

Melissa frowned. "Some what?"

"You know, some dirt, we'll spread a little dirt around, casually at first, just to make them sort of start thinking twice about rushing into anything. Right now they're just looking at each other's outer shell in a way, but there's a lot more underneath that shell, a lot more. They just don't know it yet. Our job is to educate and inform."

"You want to talk stink about our friend," said Betty.

"Only to Archie," said Harley. "No one else has to hear it."

Josh finished licking each of his fingers clean and was picking his teeth with a fork while making smacking sounds. "It's for a good cause."

Melissa watched him for a second, the word hog

came to mind, while a vision of them all getting together for more of these greasy dinners until they were old and gray, and she suddenly leaned forward towards Harley, very interested. "What kind of dirt?"

"You know, something real that we know about the other person, nothing that's made up otherwise it'll seem fake and won't work. Let's start with our buddy Archie. He's a good for nothing playboy with a lot of names in that little black book of his."

"He takes secret trips and never tells anyone where he goes," said Bob.

"He's a poor sport, and a bad loser," said Josh.

"He's always late," said Bob, "no matter what the situation,"

"He drives a gas guzzling truck," said Josh, "and his carbon footprint is bigger than an average county. He's whiny and.."

"He cheats," said Bob.

Josh looked at Bob. "He cheats?"

"Yeah," Bob turned to Josh, "remember that one time he brought a pitching wedge to the course that had square grooves? They've been banned for years, and he pretended like he didn't know the rule. Yeah, right."

Betty laughed. "What, are you guys on the PGA tour now?"

They ignored her and continued slandering Archie. Josh slammed the table. "Yeah and what about that time it was raining and he was missing a lot of short putts, and he changed the grip on his putter in the middle of the round, wrapped it with some tacky tape to give him a better grip, right there on the fifth hole, clearly a rules violation. You cannot adjust a club in the middle of a round."

"Always trying to get one up on us on the course, that bastard."

"Why do we even play golf with that guy?"

Betty put her hands up. "Okay, okay, we get it. He cheats at golf. I don't think that's going to make Marlena think twice about going to Paris with him."

"Any guy that cheats at golf will cheat at everything else," said Bob knowingly.

"I think we'll just stick with the little black book for starters," said Betty, "so he's had a lot of girlfriends?"

"Hundreds," said Josh.

Bob nodded. "Could be thousands for all we know."

"Thousands? Really Bob?" said Angie.

"Alright, he's had a few, maybe a dozen that we know about." Bob was counting on his fingers, thinking hard.

"That's not really abnormal is it, for you guys I mean?" said Betty. Her eyes burned ice as she looked over at Harley, and he slid the sunglasses back down. "Okay," she said, "so we'll push the whole playboy issue. He's never on time and he likes to play the field. Not a real responsible type of guy, no one she wants to get serious with anyways."

"Now, we're kind of in a bind here," said Melissa to Betty, "because they know everything about Archie, but we don't know anything about Marlena, nothing really."

"Nothing," said Bob. "Except that she's pretty dang good looking."

Angie narrowed her eyes.

"Great," said Harley. "A lot of help you'll be."

"Look," said Betty, "we might be able to pry a few tidbits from her that you can use. What does Archie like in a girl?"

"Well he obviously likes pretty Brazilian ballet dancers," said Bob.

They all watched as the two love birds danced near the band. Archie was smiling from ear to ear.

"Alright wrong question," said Betty. "What does he hate about girls? We'll work that angle, and see if we can find anything to use."

The guys wrinkled their brows, thinking hard, while the girls looked at them with disdain; Bob was still counting on his fingers, trying to add up all the girlfriends Archie had dated over the years.

Harley looked straight at Betty. "You know, he's probably a lot like most every other guy in a lot of ways. Doesn't want a controlling jealous maniac girlfriend for one thing who reads a lot into nothing, turns a mohill into a mountain, and flies off the handle for no good reason."

"No good reason?" asked Betty.

"Clingy is bad," said Josh, "very bad."

"Remember that psycho chick from Reno?" said Bob. "We all went to Tahoe one year to ski and gamble, man it was such a blast. Anyways Archie had this technique, said he'd perfected it, where he'd be waiting in line for the chair lift up the mountain, and when he saw a good looker waiting back in the pack he'd make eye contact and yell out 'single!' and she'd come forward to join him on the ride up the mountain, he'd get to know her and ask her out. That guy's got all the angles."

"Does this story have an ending anytime soon?" said Angie impatiently.

"Yeah, and not a very good one. Anyways, he takes this girl to dinner that night, realizes that even though she's drop dead gorgeous, she's a wacko, so he ditches her after paying the bill, and escapes out the side door. We all jump on the plane the next day and when Archie gets home; there she is waiting on his *doorstep*, holding a bouquet of flowers."

"Creepy."

"She says she looked everywhere for him after their dinner and was worried something might have happened to him, tracked him down using just his name and took the first flight in the morning just to be with him, said she wanted to be with him *forever,* just like in that ghost movie. He called the cops and it turns out she had a warrant for assault back in Reno, beat up her boyfriend or something and off she went wearing cop bracelets, screaming to Archie that she loved him, to wait for her, as they were shoving her into the squad car."

Bob slapped his thigh. "I've got it! You girls can have Marlena waiting on his doorstep holding a bouquet of flowers and it'll jog a memory in his brain, kinda like the dog thing."

Angie frowned. "The dog thing Bob? Really?"

"Yeah, you know the thing where the guy rings the bell and feeds the dog and it triggers a reaction, only in this case it's a girl on a porch with flowers, and instead of wagging his tail, 'ol Archie'll pee his pants and run away as fast as he can. Man, I'd pay to see that."

Harley filed that idea away for later, he'd forgotten all about the psycho chick from Reno. He figured he could pay some random girl a few bucks to wait in the bushes on the first hole and right before Archie teed off for the round she'd bounce up and yell at Archie that she loved him and wave the flowers and then disappear. He'd be so rattled; he'd be easy money after that probably for a whole week and maybe a month or more.

The song came to an end and Harley looked over to the dance floor and could see their two friends wading back through the tables towards them.

"Okay," he said hurriedly and leaned over the table, "let's all get on the same page. You girls push the whole 'Archie is a two timing womanizing skunk who will leave her at the altar to cheat us in a round of golf, and we'll push the notion that she's a money grubbing clingy whore that will suffocate him with a pillow while he's sleeping." He pounded on the table for effect.

The girls looked at him with astonishment and their mouths agape, while the guys nodded their approval.

Betty was perturbed. "But we never said she was..."

"Work with us woman!" Harley shouted at her, and then motioned with his hands for all to remain calm as the two love birds, holding hands got closer to the table.

"And then Archie missed the putt," said Harley laughing loudly, pretending he was continuing with a funny story, "and I won the match again. Oh, hey there you two are, I was just recapping today's golf outing for the women folk."

The 'women folk' looked like a pack of angry wolves ready to leap over the table at Harley.

Archie frowned and pulled out the chair for his

date. "They don't seem too thrilled with the story Harley, it's got a bad ending."

Marlena was bubbling over with enthusiasm, and it was that brightness alone that pulled her friends out of their depressions, and the three girls managed a glimmer of a smile while looking at her.

"I just love to dance. Love, love, love it." She motioned with her graceful hands. "Girls, the dance floor is open, and wonderful I might add." And then the girls all frowned again as they looked at their hapless dates, while the guys reached for their beers and frowned just as deeply.

"Now who wants dessert?" asked Marlena cheerily.

3.

Tuesday

Harley surveyed his realm like Caesar on the battlefield. His auto repair shop was running smoothly, he had three bays to work out of, and they were all filled with jobs, and two more cars were on the side. Mason was tuning up an SUV in the right bay, revving the engine as he read the computer. Jintao was changing the struts on a van in the left bay, the steady brraaap brraaap brraaap of the pneumatic gun loosening the bolts, like music to the ears of a mechanic. The only other sounds that brought so much peace and serenity to his innermost soul, was the distinctive sound of his golf ball clunking into the hole for a birdie, and the subsequent sound of Archie sobbing in agony as he lost the match. Hopefully he'd hear that wonderful melody later in the day, but for now it was work, work, and more work.

The shop didn't make a lot of money for him after all the bills were paid at the end of each month. There was the lease rent and insurance and workers comp and wages and equipment and tools and electric and water and taxes and more taxes, and whenever he got caught up something would break, and he would need to buy new equipment. By the time he paid all the 'ands', there wasn't much left over for him except a few bucks for food, gas, beer and golf. But that was okay by Harley, he was his own boss and could come and go as he pleased, and play golf whenever he wanted. Freedom came with a price, and if that price was being perpetually broke, then so be it.

He was getting ready to drop the steering system from an old truck in the middle bay. Old man Pinkerton had brought it in early this morning and asked Harley if he could do the repair, since all the other shops in town were booked solid for a week or more. It was a tough job and they probably just didn't want to deal with the old and rusty bolts.

"You should have come to me first," said Harley. "I'd have it finished already."

"I nevah know…" the old man said. "I thought you only took care of new cars."

"Ah, that's alright, you come back in two hours and I'll have this bad boy back in action."

"Two hours, that's it?"

"I don't mess around."

Harley got on the phone and ordered the parts from the store and then started spraying lubricant on the old bolts.

He'd bought the building ten years ago, and with a lot of sweat equity had made it into a respectable establishment. He was known as an honest mechanic, honest enough that is; sure he'd mark up the price on parts by a couple of bucks, ten percent or so, but not fifty percent like some of the other shmucks around town.

Being a mechanic was a man's job, and Harley considered himself a king among mechanics. There was nothing he enjoyed more than tackling the toughest of the tough jobs, bolts that were frozen solid, parts that wouldn't fit, tools that wouldn't fit. Knuckle busting jobs. The ones no else wanted anything to do with. It was amazing how some cars were designed and engineered so that to get a bolt off from one little part you had to take half the car apart to get at it. Solving the problem was half the fun though, and he sure was going to have fun getting the steering system taken apart with this old rusty truck, and he smiled inside. Yes, he was like a General on the field ready to go to battle at eight in the morning on a Tuesday, and he knew that when noon rolled around he'd be going out to do battle of a different sort, out on the Captain's course, and that brought an end to his smile. He remembered now. It was Tuesday, and Betty would be working. He'd have to see her up in the starters' box, checking everyone in, squawking on the loudspeaker, looking like Betty.

It was eight months since she'd broken it off with him, eight long months and he reminisced about how he'd determined to carry on as though it wasn't going to be a problem. There was no talking her out of it, for she was as hard headed and thick skinned as a Galapagos turtle. He figured he'd just drink beer, play golf and race cars until the next good one came along. It had been a long wait, and he was beginning to think he'd never find another decent girl on the whole island. Golf was the ultimate escape from reality and his fellow combatants were like a support team of sorts, a deflection from his discontent and disappointment in his life. If he could beat the tar out of Archie, who was rich and successful and content with his life, then all was well. If could whip up on Bob and Josh for good measure, then it was like icing on a cake, or froth on a good beer.

He tried to date other girls; the tattooed skank from the barbershop; the physical therapist from the Y, the waitress from the Pit. He even had lunch one day with a girl on vacation who ran an actual Zoo on the mainland. His friends set him up with her as a blind date, said they'd get along just great. She turned out to be as out-front and direct as he was.

"Look," he told her when they sat down to order. "I'm not a real chit chat kind of guy okay? So let's keep this simple."

She threw her water in his face and asked sweetly, "Simple enough for you?" and walked out the door. He actually kind of liked that girl, she had a good attitude. Oh well, on to the next. No one told him life would easy after dating a girl like Bonzai Betty.

He had a great dog to keep him company and guard the shop. He was an Australian Cattle Dog and was the best damn dog Harley had ever seen. It was a strange sort of dog, a mix between dingo and terrier that the Aussies had bred around the turn of the Seventeenth century. He was short and beefy and strong with thick grey and white fur and a black ring around his ears and around his eyes that made him look like a bandit. He was smart as a whip and could kick the tarnation out of any other dog that came around. Harley named him 'Prisoner' when he got him as a puppy. "You're never getting away from me," he joked. "I'm the warden."

"That's a mean name," the therapist from the Y told him one day.

"But he likes it," said Harley, "watch." And he

started calling out his dog's name. "Here Prisoner, c'mon Prisoner." And the dog came running over wagging his tail and looking up at Harley with bright eyes. "See?"

"That's because he doesn't know what you're saying, that he's a prisoner."

"But he's not 'a prisoner', he's 'Prisoner', get it?" She was kind of dimwitted with no sense of humor and did not get it. She threw her hair over her shoulder, said something that sounded like 'Hurumph' and walked out the door never to be seen again. Oh well.

For Prisoner, being an Australian cattle dog meant that he needed a job, he couldn't lay around like some of the other lazy, no good mangy dogs around town. He was bred to work, and work hard, chasing cattle and herding them and driving them into pens from dawn to dusk. The biggest meanest most uncooperative cow would only make this type of dog more adamant to control it, and he would not give up until the cow was, well, cowed. With no cattle at the auto shop, or anywhere else nearby for that matter, Harley needed to train Prisoner to do other tasks, otherwise he might get bored and run away to find a cattle ranch or something. So he trained him to bring him tools, and pick up the trash, and chase away the chickens, and door to door salesmen, or Jehovah's Witnesses who might come to bother them while they were working on the cars. If you didn't have a car to be fixed, or weren't coming to pick up a car that was already fixed, then you would be herded away from the auto shop like cattle on a ranch by the toughest dog you'd ever seen.

The only salesmen, or should we say 'salespeople' that Prisoner would let near the shop were the door to door fundraising kids from the nearby elementary school. They always had something going on, fundraising for this or that all year long, huli-huli chicken, or chocolate bars, or pancake breakfasts, or raffles, or car washes. Prisoner would bark his happy bark and wag his tail when they'd come calling, and Harley always protested a little and bought a lot. The kids loved Prisoner, and would run around with him, petting him and throwing the stick until they got tired and needed to go back to their raising of funds, and Prisoner would just sit there by the big bay door and watch them go.

"Don't worry Prisoner," Harley would say. "Someday I'll find you a kid to play with all day long. In the meantime, go fetch me a wrench." And off he'd go.

Harley stood looking at the truck in the air, and the pending knuckle busting job. Now where is that dog, he wondered. He whistled and yelled out 'Prisoner', and sure enough that good dog came running around the corner looking for commands to follow.

"Wrench," said Harley and Prisoner ran over to his tool box and came back with a box wrench in his mouth. "Good boy," said Harley and he bent down to pet the dog on the head and wiped off the slobber with a rag from his pocket. Lumbering down the access road to the shop came a big blue truck with Bubba driving. The license plate read DMWB, for 'Don't Mess With Bubba'. Prisoner barked and ran off towards the truck. Bubba always brought snacks from the restaurant when he came in to get a repair job, and Prisoner ran next to the truck all the way to the shop, licking his chops and wagging his tail. The truck turned into the shop and parked in front of the middle bay, and Harley could clearly hear the squealing noise from the left front wheel.

Bubba got out of the truck holding a bone from a prime rib. He held it high in the air and good 'ol Prisoner sat as still as a rock, saliva dripping down the side of his jaw.

"Stay," said Bubba, obviously enjoying this. "Now roll over." And the dog rolled over twice without touching the ground, and popped back up to his sitting position, eyes steady on the prize. "Roll over... the other way." Prisoner was already halfway through his roll, and Bubba shouted, "The other way!" and he quickly righted himself and rolled over the other way. "Now walk backwards. Forward. Stand on your hind legs, now lay down." And the dog performed each task as quickly and efficiently as he could while keeping one eye on the bone to make sure it didn't disappear.

"Good boy," said Bubba. "Now go get it," and he threw the bone far away while Prisoner scampered after it. Bubba had learned his lesson long ago, don't hand Prisoner a bone, he'll likely take a finger along with it.

"Left front, right?" asked Harley. He liked joking with people more than anything, even giants who could squash him like a bug.

"Right," said Bubba.

"Right front?" asked Harley.

Bubba frowned. "What?"

"Left front, or right front."

"It's the left front Harley."

"Ha-ha, I was just messing with you Bubba."

"You see this license plate on my truck? You know what it says don't you?"

"Yeah, yeah, DMWB, don't mess with Bubba. C'mon man, it's too early in the morning to be so serious."

Harley wheeled over a jack stand and pumped the front corner off the ground, and then with a couple of brrraaappp brrraaappps from the pneumatic wrench had the wheel off in flash. He pulled the outer bearing off the axle and took a quick look. "Yep, the bearing is shot. See take a look."

"I have no idea what to look for," said Bubba. "You're the mechanic, just fix it."

"We should really change all four wheel bearings at the same time; it'll save you money in the long run."

Harley noticed the frown on Bubba's face.

"Or you can just wait until you hear a squealing noise and a wheel falling off in the middle of the road. Funny thing though, how it was just the left front making all the noise."

"What do you mean funny?"

"Well, you see, just the front left bearing wore out enough to make that noise, and it's funny since that's where most of the weight of the car is located, and that's what made it wear out quicker than the rest."

"What do you mean where most of the weight is located?"

"How much do you weigh?"

Bubba made a fist and flexed his bicep. "About three fifty and counting, why?"

"That's ten percent of the weight of the whole truck. These things were designed for an average driver in the two hundred pound range Bubba. You're a little bit, how do I say this, 'above average'."

Bubba smiled at that, it actually made him happy. "I am above average. You know it takes a lot of work to get this big."

"And a lot of food."

"I like you Harley, my brother doesn't, but I think you're okay."

"I'm not gonna worry about it. Probably has something to do with the drag races on the west side, what do you think are the chances, huh Bubba? I guess I wouldn't like it either if I was getting beat to the finish line all the time."

"Before you got back from overseas, he was winning a lot out there. Now nothing. He thinks you're cheating."

"Tell him to drive faster. It's not always the car, sometimes it's the driver. You gotta be fast on the shift. Third gear wins the race."

"I don't know nothin' about racin'. I'm a bouncer. That's what I'm good at. You mess up and I get my hands on you, I bounce you out the door like a basketball." Bubba pointed at the apple green car in one of the bays. "That your dragster?"

"Yeah, come check it out." The hood was up on the Camaro, the engine gleaming silver. "Big block four fifty, I tweaked it a bit, bored out the pistons to get it up to nearly five hundred, racing cam, dual four barrel carbs, nitro…"

"Whoa, whoa whoa… you lost me at big block Harley. Damn you sound like my brother."

Prisoner, gnawing on the bone by the wall, looked towards the road and growled; he jumped up and stood there with the hair sticking up along his back.

"What's gotten into that dog?" muttered Harley.

A big black SUV with tinted windows turned off the main highway and was coming slowly down the driveway. The license plate read LETHAL II.

'What's with these guys and their vanity plates?' thought Harley.

"It's Manini, I told him to give me a ride," said Bubba.

"That explains it," said Harley as they watched the truck approach. Prisoner sure was a smart dog.

One day when he was just a pup and Harley took him to the golf course he walked right over and peed on Manini's tire. Everyone thought it was funny except for Manini who chased Prisoner through the parking lot with a three iron. That guy sure had a bad attitude, and a bad habit of chasing people and puppies with golf clubs. Lucky for Manini that the little pup was quick enough to get away, because Harley had one hand on a pipe wrench if one little dog hair of his Prisoner was harmed. One rule in life is that you don't mess with someone else's dog. When the pup was safe in the bushes Harley took a hose from the cart shack and in a gesture of goodwill hosed off the offended tire. Another rule in life is that you don't mess with someone else's car, unless they deserve it that is.

Manini pulled up to them and he leaned out the window and snarled at Prisoner. Prisoner snarled back and started barking, Manini barked back. It went on and on, neither one backing down, eyes locked in battle, barking away at each other.

Bubba looked over at Harley and shook his head. "The little brother."

Manini stopped barking for a moment and shouted out to Harley as he revved the engine. "Check it out Harley, big block Chevy! Gonna kick your ass on the track!" He kept revving the engine, the deep rumble of the pistons firing and echoing through the auto shop bays. The other mechanics stopped what they were doing to listen; poking their heads out from under the cars they were working on, nodding their approval at the raw power of the engine.

"I'll see you later Harley," said Bubba. "Call me when it's done. I gotta get him out of here before he burns up a tank of gas just sitting there. I just hope he gets it in the right gear this time." Bubba waved at Manini with a fist and a grunt to cut it out and snarled at him as he got in truck, which even though was an extra large model settled on its suspension as big Bubba sat down.

"Hey, where'd that dog go?" shouted Manini out the window. He looked at all his side and rear view mirrors but couldn't see 'ol Prisoner at the back of the car taking care of business on the inside of the rear tire.

Harley shrugged his shoulders as Prisoner shook his leg and then trotted proudly back to his spot by the wall without looking back, having made his point on the offender. Manini barked out of his window again but Prisoner ignored him and went back to gnawing on his steak bone. The ultimate insult from a dog is when it doesn't even acknowledge your presence. Manini made a slow three point turn, the rubber on the big tires squealing as they turned on the concrete, and then, when he was pointed towards the exit, he punched the accelerator to the floorboard and burned rubber down the driveway until Bubba popped him up alongside his head.

Harley held his breath in the middle of the cloud of black exhaust and rubber until finally a gust of wind cleared the air. "Good boy Prisoner," he said as he exhaled, and got to work on the two cars. Within a couple of hours he had both jobs finished, road tested, parked and ready for pickup next to the office.

Jintao sauntered over while wiping the grease off his hands. He had a worried look. "So Harley, are we gonna get paid this week?" He smiled hopefully.

"Yeah, about that," Harley motioned for him to follow and he led him into the office. "Have a seat." Harley plopped into a chair behind the metal desk, pulled out a timesheet, and a check book and started punching numbers on a calculator.

"My wife," said Jintao, "she's all over me, says I should get paid in full for all the time owed or find another garage to work at. But I like it here Harley, you're a good boss, you treat us well, this shop is clean and organized, and well, I don't want to leave."

"I know, I know," said Harley, "it's your wife. Remember what I always told you about wives."

"What's that?"

"They're always right."

Jintao laughed. "You sure know women Harley. That's probably why you never got married eh?"

Harley waved his forefinger at Jintao. "From my point of view, and this is just me okay, I've got to be right once in a while, it's just the way I am, and from everything I've seen, a happy life is a happy wife, and a happy wife is the one who's always right, so in my case it doesn't work." He went back to calculating, punching in numbers. "So let's see, I owe you the past two weeks, eighty hours equals two thousand and change. How about I write you a check for eight hundred right now, and I'll do the payroll and pay you in full by the end of this week?"

The mechanic shuffled his feet and looked at the ground. "I don't know Harley, my wife…"

"Alright, thirteen hundred, just till the end of the week." He noted the disappointed look on Jintao's face, it was borderline fear, and he knew why. Jintao's wife outweighed him by a hundred pounds or more, and was probably eating him out of house and home, and if he didn't bring home some more food really soon he'd be in big trouble. "Look, I have to get paid for these jobs first in order to pay you. This is how a business works, they pay me, I pay you and everybody else. It's in one hand and out the other every week, I don't have a magic bank account full of cash."

Jintao nodded. "Okay, but you're sure you can pay the rest by Friday?"

"Scouts honor." Harley was already writing the check and quickly ripped it out of the ledger and handed it over the desk before Jintao could change his mind. "Now once you're done with the van struts get hopping on the other two cars in line.

Chop chop."

As Jintao left the office Harley looked over the ledger and sighed. Now he was overdrawn. He could only hope that either Jintao's wife would wait till tomorrow morning to cash the check, or that the jobs being done today would pay in cash by the end of the day and he could hustle it to the bank before they closed. Sometimes they would delay cashing checks he wrote until the next day or two if they saw he was overdrawn. He had good connections at the bank, and they wanted to make sure his business thrived and didn't go belly up leaving them with a mortgage note and pennies on the dollar rather than dollars on the dollars.

Harley looked at the framed photographs on the wall, and reminisced. There he was with his unit, full dress uniform, and another with his platoon on patrol in the desert, hamming it up for the camera in between jobs, finding and destroying munitions, defusing roadside bombs. He'd started out in the mechanical division, repairing tanks and trucks and pretty much anything with a motor that moved, it was good fun, but then he moved into demolitions to get closer to the action and got to blow things up, buildings and munitions, and booby traps, front line stuff. The danger zone. The place upon which everything else in life that came after was weighed heavily against. Purposely putting yourself in harm's way on the battlefield to save lives and not get blown up in the process. He missed his squad mates, but not the work.

There was another photo below all the rest at eye level, black in white. The General of the Army came to visit them in the field, boost in moral and all that, and brought along his staff photographer who gave them all a copy, a real whiz kid, he said that black and white gave the photos a timeless appeal or some such rubbish, and that it did. A snapshot frozen in time. There was the General and him and a couple of the guys from the bomb squad, Jimmy and Mick, and Jose. Smiling big for the camera, in their desert fatigues, big guns in hand, bullet belts over their shoulders. Mick didn't make it, he bought the big house in the sky later that same day, his smile in the picture although black and white, was in reality vibrant and alive, and what he'd remember the most, a hero to the end. He hadn't heard from Jimmy and Jose in a long time, they were lost somewhere in the States. The General got busted for having an affair on Uncle Sam's dime, got his hand caught in someone else's cookie jar, the perks of power gone to his head. He was thrown out on his ear, and last he heard was shoveling manure for some of the politicians in D.C.

After Mick bought it, Harley didn't want to be in the service anymore and when his tour was up he came home for good.

Being a veteran, and especially one that got sent to the front lines of a battle zone got some perks when it came time to acquire credit, but that credit still needed to be paid, and it was times like this, usually at the beginning or the end of the month when it was crunch time, as in his wallet getting crunched, when he wondered if it was all worth it. Maybe he should just forget about trying to be an entrepreneur and go out and get a steady eddy job and let someone else worry about the red tape.

He looked at his watch and his face lightened

up, it was eleven o'clock, almost game time, and he rubbed his hands together and smiled. "I'm gonna beat the living tar out of Archie today." Suddenly the day was looking brighter. He pulled out his cell phone and dialed him up.

"What do you mean Josh doesn't want to play today?" asked Harley. On the other end of the phone line was Archie.

"That's what he told me when I called him after breakfast, said he was feeling kind of tired, stayed up all night watching some sort of drama show marathon."

"Drama show marathon?"

"Yep."

"What the hell kind of drama show can you watch all night?"

"I don't know," said Archie, "but it sure must have been a good one."

"Said he was tired huh?"

"Yep, too tired to play golf, imagine that."

"Call him back, tell him to get his rear end in gear and get to the course or we're coming up there to drag him out of his house."

"I tried, he's not answering his phone now, he must have unplugged it."

"It's Tuesday," said Harley, "one of the best days of the week to play the game."

"I know, it's a damn shame. Guess we'll just have to play without him."

"Not a chance," said Harley, "he'll be there. You let me take care of this. Just be at the course at the usual time, and I'll make sure 'ol Josher boy gets out bed. Drama show hell, I'll give him some drama. Try to get out of the game will he."

"What are you gonna do?"

"Never mind, just be at the course," said Harley and hung up the phone.

4.

Josh lived on the outskirts of town on the bottom floor of a duplex that he rented from a retired cop and his wife, who spent half their time 'travelling' as they called it, but in reality spent half the year in Vegas, living in cheap luxurious hotels and plowing through the buffet lines around town. They liked the action, and it was a good set up for Josh because he got the run of the house most of the year. He got the place practically rent free, all he had to do was take care of the yard and do some fixing up, painting and what not once in a while. The problem was that when the cop and his wife were travelling, Josh let it all hang out so to speak.

Harley pulled up in front of the house and frowned. "What a mess." The grass was un-mowed and a foot tall, beer cans piled up next to the door, clothes hanging from lampposts, but the worst for Harley was seeing the tools scattered haphazardly around the garage. "Looks like a damn slum."

The old lady next door, Mrs. Ching, kept her house and yard clean as a whistle, the lawn freshly mowed, flowering plants placed in perfect proportion to the house. She had a large eighty pound bull terrier chained to the fence out front for protection, and normally it was a menacing beast ready to growl, bark, rip, bite and tear at a moment's notice, but not today. It wagged its tail ferociously, jumping up and down and acting like a giant eighty pound puppy. His name was 'Chompers', and he was best buddies with Prisoner who was also jumping around in the back of Harley's truck wagging his tail like it might come off. When they were both puppies Harley used to bring Prisoner over and let him play with Chompers, they'd race each other and scrapple and sniff around the yards together, and they were still the best of buddies.

"Stay," said Harley to Prisoner as he got out of the truck and surveyed the scene. "It's like a damn crime scene. How in the hell can someone live like this?" He gave Prisoner a biscuit treat, and told him again to stay, and the Aussie sat down obediently in the bed of the truck. Harley walked over to the still wiggling Chompers and gave him his own little biscuit treat and petted his massive head. "Good boy Chompers, atta boy, good doggie, now come with me." He took the dog off the chain and while holding onto the collar led him towards Josh's house.

Now Chompers hated Josh with a passion. He growled and barked and strained to get off his chain to bite him every time he saw him, and had managed to get a hold of him a couple of times, and Josh had the scars to prove it. There was nothing Josh could do to get the dog to like him. He tried feeding him steaks, and treats, and any kind of yummy dog biscuits he could find but it was to no avail. It was a heck of a thing to have a dog like that live right next door to you and want to tear you to pieces any time he saw you, but after all it was Josh's own fault.

When the dogs were a couple of years old, and what you would consider their teenage years and not quite all the way grown into their feet, the cop and his wife had a Fourth of July party at the house and everyone was there. They drank and barbecued and had a great old time. Mrs. Ching from next door was there along with all the golfing buddies and half the town. Long strings of firecrackers were going off all over the neighborhood, and the dogs were cowering in the corner from the noise. For some stupid reason Josh lit a single small firecracker and threw it close to them, and Chompers thought it was a biscuit treat and got a little too close to it before it blew up in his face, and he chased Josh around the yard nipping at his heels while everyone at the party laughed and laughed. It was the highlight of the year, and folks talked about it to this day, Josh tossing the firecracker and getting chased. Problem was, Chompers remembered it too, and now he was twice as big, and twice as mean.

"Good doggy," soothed Harley as he led him towards Josh's door. "Good boy." The wagging tail was slowly diminishing, and being replaced by a low and menacing growl as they got closer to the door. Chompers could smell his enemy's presence.

Harley looked in the window and could see Josh asleep on the couch on the far side of the living room, empty beer cans and pizza boxes were scattered on the floor.

"Time to wake up," whispered Harley, and he reached under the mat and found the key and slowly opened the door a crack and ushered a confused Chompers in, and just before he shut the door locking the dog inside he reached into his pocket and pulled out a small string of firecrackers, lit the fuse and threw it towards the couch and slammed the door and ran.

5.

Archie got off the phone with Harley and continued watching the television screen with great interest.

He had no idea how Harley was going to get Josh out of the house, and for that matter he didn't really care, he had bigger fish to fry. He was in his air conditioned workout room in his home that looked out over the pool, and was trying to mimic the movements that were being demonstrated on the video. On the ceiling above him were giant stainless steel rings, and hanging from them were thick rubber bands leading to handles that he was pulling and pushing on, twisting and rotating his body against the steady resistance of the rubber.

"Now as you can see…" the voice on the video was saying, "…as you rotate your inner core, and extend your arms out with the resistance bands holding you back, you're building the power that you need to increase your distance off the tee…" twist, push, "…and as you pull back against the tension, you're building the power that you need for control…" twist, pull, "…power and control, power and control…"

Even though the temperature of the room was a steady sixty five degrees, Archie was sweating from head to toe. He'd been working out since dawn, getting ready for the day, getting ready for the golf match. Harley had been taking all the matches for the past several weeks; in fact Archie couldn't ever remember the last time he'd won. But that was all going to change very soon. He was taking secret lessons from the pro on the other side of the island; he had this workout video, new golf balls, new spikes, a new diet, and a new girlfriend. Speaking of whom, was down at the pool at this moment getting a tan and looking fine, he could see her stretched out next to the blue water.

He gave one last push on the bungee, turned off the DVD, and took a couple of practice swings with an imaginary golf club and watched his imaginary golf ball fly straight down the imaginary fairway.

"You're going down Harley."

At the pool Marlena sat in a lounge chair next to an umbrella reading a trashy novel. She wore a large wide brimmed hat and giant white sunglasses. Harley walked down the steps, gave a wolf whistle, and she smiled and waved.

"Enjoying yourself?" He asked as he sat down next to her.

She folded her book. "I feel like a movie star on vacation."

"You sure look the part." He poured a glass of iced tea and sat back in the shade of the umbrella.

"Had a good workout?" She asked.

"Excellent. It's tailored specifically for a golf swing, I'm gonna hit the goldurn cover off that ball today."

"Is that good?"

"It's just a saying; I'm not actually going to hit the cover off of it. I think that's impossible actually. What I'm trying to do is get more power."

"You should take ballet lessons."

"What?"

"Yes, I think it would help you gain more power through balance. Ballet dancers are very powerful because they have great balance."

His brow furrowed as he considered it, and then he laughed. "Not a chance. Can you imagine the grief the other guys would give me if they ever found out?"

"It would give you more flexibility and strength in your upper torso and legs. I think it would definitely help your golf game."

"Really?" That gave him reason to pause for a nanosecond, and then he had a clear vision of himself getting ready to hit the ball on the first tee, and having Harley toss a tutu next to his feet, grinning with an all knowing smile, as he sliced the ball out of bounds. He shuddered, "No, I really don't want to take ballet lessons, but thank you for asking."

"I read once where players in the NFL have taken ballet lessons and have done quite well."

"Name one."

She thought hard for a moment. "Lynn Swan. I remember his name because of one of the most famous ballet's in the world; Swan Lake."

He frowned. "Lynn Swan. Of the Pittsburgh Steelers. Took ballet."

"I'm certain of it, and there were many, many more once they found out, since he was so successful, at football that is. In fact I read where some coaches even made ballet mandatory for the whole team, because of that one player. So there."

Archie was silent for a moment while he took it all in, and then nodded, all-knowing. "Okay, well, I can see where it 'could' work for football players; heck, if someone tried to rib you about taking ballet; you could just tackle 'em and shove their head in the dirt, break their face, and a couple of other bones while you're at it. Golf is different; it is way, WAY harder than football, let me tell you. If someone's ribbing you about something, you know, getting under your skin, needling you, well you just have to grin and bear it and take it like a man, since it's as much a part of the game as actually hitting the ball." He made a scoffing sound. "Golf is way harder than football, I can goldurn guarantee you that."

"So no ballet?"

He smiled. "Okay, okay, I'll take some private lessons, but no tutu."

She hit him on the knee with her book. "If you think golf is hard, you'll be crying after I get done with you."

"I'm not going to have to stand on the tips of my toes am I?"

"No, but after doing a couple of hundred arches you won't be able to walk the next day without wincing, I can goldurn guarantee you that mister."

"Alright, well I gotta get going, it's almost noon. Should we meet for dinner again tonight?"

"Not tonight, I have ballet with the girls."

"What about tomorrow night?"

She smiled. "Yes."

He was hopeful. "Alone?"

She was firm. "No. I just love it when we have our friends with us. Please sweetie?"

"I'm not sure they love it. This plan is insane. You really think this is going to work don't you?"

She was excited. "I can see it in their eyes Archie; they really want to be back together, in their hearts. All we have to do is to keep inviting them out with us, trick them any which way we can to be in the same building with each other, and they will gravitate back to each other. It's like the moon and the earth, they are circling each other, around and around, but sooner or later gravity will win, and they will be back together again."

"The moon and the earth, getting back together. That's how you equate this whole scenario playing out?"

"It will happen, eventually. Gravity is the most powerful force in the universe, besides love."

"Have you ever seen a shooting star? A little flick in the sky is all that is. Some of them are no bigger than a grain of sand. The moon and earth getting back together will be an explosion that will rock the solar system."

"My point exactly."

His eyes narrowed. She always seemed to have a smart response. "Okay, but I'm telling you right now, you're playing with forces of which you have no idea how large and powerful and ornery, and well, downright mean they can be." And then he wagged his finger at her. "But you know I got to tell you, your analogy of the moon and earth crashing into each other sounds about right, especially with Betty and Harley. It's really more like two freight trains loaded with bombs heading towards each other on the same track, but the earth and moon work too. The only thing that concerns me is that you and me live on the Earth."

While heading down the steps towards the garage and trying to think of a good fake injury angle to try for a stroke or two advantage from Harley, he nearly stepped on his cat, Mr. Whiskers and tumbled the remaining steps to the bottom, and held his knee in real pain.

6.

"Princess Hotel Concierge, may I help you?"

The deep voice on the other end was polite yet firm. "I want to book a tee time."

Melissa sat up straighter than normal in her chair at the front of the hotel. The voice on the phone sounded gentle and kind and very much in control. She imagined a business man on vacation, dressed in a suit and tie, clean shaven, aftershave cologne, slick hair, shoes shined, clothes pressed and arranged neatly in the closet, a steady high paying job.

"Why certainly sir, there are three courses nearby, would you like to hear the options, or do you already know which one you'd like to play?"

"I hate to trouble you," he said, "but could you tell me the options? I've never been here before."

"Why it would be no trouble at all!" said Melissa her voice skipping a little bit along with her heart as she pulled out the golf course price sheet. He was polite, *and* considerate, he'd never been here before and didn't want to trouble her. Silly man. It would be no trouble at all. She trembled a little as she imagined him stepping out of the elevator, dressed in brand new golf clothes and shoes, making direct eye contact with her, knowing immediately that it was her that he had talked to, and falling deeply and passionately in love at first sight. She read off the prices for the courses near the hotel, it was high season and all were in the hundred and fifty dollar to two hundred dollar range, surely he would laugh at the prices and ask her which course she'd prefer to play, and maybe even tell her to take the day off and join him.

There was silence on the other end of the phone for a moment and she had to ask if he was still there.

"Yes, I'm still here. I heard that there's another course nearby, somewhere up on the hill they tell me, that's more, how do we say, reasonable."

And just like that her heart sank like a rock. Reasonable meant cheap, as in cheapskate, and her vision of the person on the other end changed without warning.

"Well, yes there is another course nearby, but it's only nine holes..." She still had hope.

"Well, what kind of shape is it in?"

In her mind she saw an overgrown cow pasture with pigs running around oinking at each other, and wallowing in the mud.

"Honestly, it's nowhere near the quality of the other courses."

"But can you tell me the price?"

"It's ten dollars to play all day."

"What do you mean by that?"

"It's ten dollars to walk the course, the nine holes all day long as many rounds as you want, however it's ten dollars to rent a riding cart per nine holes, so eighteen holes would cost ten dollars for the green fees, and the cart would be twenty, so in essence you're paying thirty dollars to play a nine hole course twice." Still hopeful.

"Well that sounds pretty good," he said cheerfully. "I don't need a cart, I can just walk."

And just like that all hope was gone. She imagined a vagabond walking golfer with holes in his pants and socks carrying a dirty bag with a stick over his back like a hobo walking along the tracks, followed by a swarm of flies. How could they even let someone like that into the hotel in the first place.

"Go ahead and book a tee time for me at ten this morning," said the bum.

"I'm sorry sir," said Melissa sweetly, "they don't' take tee times, it's first come first serve." Just like at the greasy spoon fast food restaurant you'll probably ask me about next, she thought. Her finger hovered over the hang up quick button, and asked, "Will there anything else?"

"Why no, you've been quite helpful…"

"Thank you for calling the concierge desk, please let us know if we can be of service in the future," she said faster than a speed reader at a coffee shop, and 'click'.

She pretended that she was washing her hands under her desk, washing that call right out of her life.

She had a small discreet mirror set up in the crook between the phone and the ledge and she checked her hair, it was up in a bun today to showcase her high cheekbones, and she was wearing black rimmed faux reading glasses to make her look studious and smart. Being the concierge at the Princess Hotel meant being practically perfect in every way and she smiled at that since she definitely looked the part.

How dare that guest waste her time quizzing her on the golf offerings in the area and then settle on that barbarian course. And how Betty could withstand working up there was beyond her and she'd tried many times without success at getting her to work with her at the hotel full time.

The more she thought about it, golf itself was a mindless, brainless game and a bizarre waste of time, but up on the Captain's course it was the devil.

When she first met Josh he seemed so fun and alive, responsible even. But as time and the years passed it seemed like he sank into some sort of dark spell, drinking and playing golf, and then drinking after golf while talking and complaining about golf. There was no room for her to even get a word in edgewise.

A bellhop strolled by pushing a load of suitcases to the elevator. He smiled and winked at her and she smiled back.

"Morning Melissa, see you in the cafeteria for lunch?"

"Maybe," she replied sweetly, and when he was past her she murmured, 'in your dreams bellboy."

And then she thought about Josh and shuddered. He looked like a bum last night at the Cave.

It all started about a year ago when Harley got back from the war. The guys played golf once in a while when he was gone, but when he got back it was all the time, every day, like an addiction, and then when Betty broke it off with him the trouble started.

Maybe it was Harley, she thought. He was the devil, getting them all riled up to play golf every day, like a drug pusher. Golf was the drug, Harley was the evil drug devil pusher man, and the Captain's course was the stinking opium den where they lost their souls on a daily basis, and then had a harder and harder time each day to come back to reality.

"Hmmm…" she thought to herself as she tapped a pencil on the desk, " well, that's it in a nutshell."

And then she saw a man and his family come

out of the elevator. The kids and the wife were all dressed for the pool and swimming, while the man was dressed in a golf shirt, golf shorts, and carrying golf shoes. He kissed them all and walked towards the Porte cochre. Smiling, while walking away from his family. The little boy was pulling at his mother's hand, he wanted to go with his Daddy, but he was walking away. It's not Harley, she thought. It's golf. That man is leaving his beautiful family behind to play a stupid game. Proof positive that golf is the devil. Without it there would be so much more happiness in the world.

Her blood began to boil at the very thought of the word golf. And then she saw her face again in the mirror and it sort of shocked her since it was her bad and angry face and she breathed deep and slow, letting the anger go out of her with each breath just like her yoga instructor taught her. In with the good, out with the bad, and she closed her eyes to further the soothing, calming result. In with the good air and out with the bad, she breathed in very deeply and slowly while envisioning calming cooling wind, golden in color and form, and as she exhaled just as slowly outward, she envisioned angry hot air and thoughts leaving her forever, and she whispered ever so softly as she exhaled, 'golf's the devil', to rid herself of that angry bad thought, and when she was satisfied that the bad thoughts were nearly depleted she took a super deep breath and while exhaling with that last thought leaving her mind, eyes still closed, she didn't see the scuba instructor from the pool come up behind her, who noticed that she was doing slow breathing exercises and tapped her gently on the shoulder and whispered into her ear, "Good job."

Which scared the living daylights out of her and

she jumped out of her chair screaming out "Golf's the devil!" The giant lobby got very quiet indeed, and when everyone looked towards her fast reddening face, she slowly slid under the desk to hide.

7.

The Hawaiians lived on the island for thousands of years, over fifty generations with no outside influence other than the occasional visit from their Polynesian cousins in the southern islands of Tahiti and Moorea. The cousins brought new idols and caught up on old news. Sometimes there was the occasional skirmish, some pushing and shoving for control, but basically they all lived in peace and harmony, with a little bit of savage war sprinkled in now and then to keep everyone honest. They were generally good natured, down to earth fun loving folk who liked to work hard, party hard, and eat lots of good food. They were responsible for two of the greatest inventions that mankind has ever seen, surfing, and the luau.

Round about the Sixteenth century the Europeans discovered the island chain and named it after the Earl of Sandwich. Unfortunately the Europeans didn't bring sandwiches, they brought a disease called smallpox for which the islanders had no immune system, and it decimated the population. Armies once vast and powerful were now small and easily managed by ships full of sailors and marines with guns. The sugar barons arrived and took over vast tracks of level land. Sugar plantations popped up all over the island and the new owners of the land, needing workers for the fields began importing hungry people from far and wide. They brought them in from China, the Philippines, Portugal, and Japan.

Pretty soon there were so many different people

speaking so many different languages that it was hard to get any work done. No one could understand without hand signals what the other guy was saying. Fistfights broke out, and it was a mess. Eventually a polyglot language emerged, based on English, which the plantation overlords spoke and insisted on, mixed with important bits and pieces of all the other languages. A mish mash of sounds called 'Pidgin English' was invented, found nowhere else in the world. It sounds something like this:

"Eh brah, you goin hit dat ball, or you goin sit on you o'kole all day?"

Translation: "Hey friend, are you going to hit the ball, or do you plan on sitting on your fanny all day?"

Most people can speak proper English and switch back and forth between Pidgin and proper whenever the situation calls for it. For instance, if you were applying for a job as a bank manager you would shelve the Pidgin and bust out your best proper English. On the other hand if you found yourself down at the local beach with a gang of tough mokes, then using the proper English would get you a proper thrashing and you'd best bring out the best braddah braddah Pidgin you can muster. It's a good idea to have a mastery of both languages.

Pretty soon after the common ground language of Pidgin was formed, and the people could communicate, the different races began to mingle and mesh, and intermarry and have kids, and suddenly you had the 'hapas' running all over the place. 'Hapa' is Hawaiian for 'half', as in half race this, have race that, and the all of the resulting whatevahs. Chinese, Hawaiian, Portuguese

Hawaiian, etc. The Hawaiian part always came last in the name since it had such a nice ring to it. That worked for about one generation, and then suddenly you had Chinese Filipino Japanese Portuguese Hawaiians running around, and all bets were off the table.

Bonzai Betty was of a particular three part mix of ethnicity that is found quite frequently on the island; Chinese, Portuguese, and Hawaiian, and showed a little bit of each distinct trait. The Chinese otherwise known as Pake in the Pidgin language were hard working, and extremely money wise, devious in some ways at saving and making money, some would say downright stingy, and they looked down on those that did not hold that trait as a shining (as in money) example in their own lives. The Portuguese were known as tough as nails fighters, excellent cowboys, great friends to one and all, saints and sinners, priests and robbers, and the best talkers that mankind has ever seen. Start a conversation with a Potcho and you'd better pull up a chair, because you'll soon be laughing at all their jokes, be amazed at all the insights they have on life, and it might be days before you can pull yourself away. The Hawaiians were mostly pure of heart, with much of their soul still grounded in the perfect land around them, physically magnificent, strong and ready for either a good round of work, or a nap under a shady tree, quick with a bright smile or a fist, take your pick.

She got the Banzai part of her name while in kindergarten and it stuck like white on rice. Without an ounce of Japanese heritage and going to a school where half the class had a Japanese last name really got her riled up, and she figured she'd do something about it.

During recess they'd all get to play outside and one of the top games was soccer. Being little kids they hadn't learned the finer art of passing the ball and they'd all bunch up around it like a school of fish. Betty would come charging in from the side yelling 'Bonzai!' at the top of her lungs and scatter the other kids like a bowling ball scattering pins. She was a tough kid from the start.

Being part Pake, Betty had three jobs, and loved to make money. This aspect of her genetic makeup was sometimes most evident when she was working at her job at the golf course. The game of golf she felt, was for old retired people who were too ancient to hold a job, and little kids who were too young to work. Sure, she played the game when she was young, and had fun at it, but that was then and this was now, and there was no extra time in the now for playing games. Grown men, many of them far from retirement age, taking time off from work to hit a little ball around a cow field got less than any respect from her. She'd take their money of course, and happy to do so as the cashier/starter at the golf course, but respect? Not one ounce.

An elderly couple from the mainland was checking in for a round of golf, and handed the money to Betty who cheerfully gave them their change. "You're third up Mr. and Mrs. Bentley, have a nice game," she said sweetly with a smile that warmed their hearts.

"Thank you dear," said Mrs. Bentley, and as they were heading down the stairway to their cart she remarked to her husband, "I just love the Hawaiian people, they are so friendly."

Mr. Roi, the golf course superintendent came up the stairs and smiled at Betty as he headed into the shop. Every golf course needs a Mr. Roi, able to fix any irrigation leak, spot a turf eating fungus from a mile away, and build good employee relations or an elevated tee box with equal ease. He was also like a favorite uncle to all the workers and gave Betty the job when she was eleven years of age, sweeping out the cart barn almost exactly fifteen years ago.

"Busy day eh Miss Betty?"

"It's a good day Mr. Roi, eighty five golfers so far."

"Terrible, terrible shame about the cart shack burning down yesterday."

"That was bad. What did the insurance people say?"

"Three months minimum to rebuild. We'll get the construction bids this week and get at it. But you know how it is around here, slow as molasses is fast as we gonna get dat money. We'll just have to deal with keeping the golf carts in a tent for a while."

"Like camping out."

"Just like camping out. Too bad the new security camera wasn't up and running, we could have caught the event on tape." He tapped on the machine. "That would have been something to see."

"Yeah, too bad about that," said Betty and her eyes narrowed. When she got to work before dawn this morning she checked the doorframe, and sure enough the scotch tape she'd put on the bottom of the frame was torn. Someone had broken in alright, but apparently taken nothing except for the tape in the security camera recorder, the empty tape. Funny how no one was really aware of the security camera, and how when she mentioned it to Harley last night he seemed so interested.

"So it's Tuesday Betty, three more days till the weekend," said Mr. Roi.

"Here we go. Tell me again Mr. Roi, what does that word mean, weekend?"

"Very funny Betty. Are you still working at the stables?"

She smiled. "Every morning before I get here."

"How you find the energy for it all I have no idea. But you're young, so do it while you can. Are you working tonight at the restaurant? Maybe I'll take the missus out."

"Oh no, I only work there on the weekend, I'm off on week nights."

"You take nights off?" Mr. Roi pretended to fall backwards holding his chest.

"Tuesday nights I dance ballet."

"You still dance ballet? I did not know that." He sat back on a stool and sighed as he reminisced. "I still remember when all you girls were little, and at the old dance studio with Mrs. Nikita, kindergarteners in your little tutus, heading to ballet class. I heard the new studio is top notch, all shiny and air conditioned, new floors, mirrored windows, just what was needed for all the new rich folks to feel safe to send their kids to dance. That old studio was so run down, but had a lot of heart. "

"Sagging floors, termite eaten beams, rusty nails…" she said. "It was still so much fun to go there."

"My daughter, well, she's quite a bit older than you, and is so busy with those boys of hers, three boys can you believe it? I should tell her to check it out; she might want to start up again."

"Well, I actually just started again, about a month ago. There's a new dance instructor from Brazil. She's really good, and I had some free time so…"

Mr. Roi snapped his fingers. "I almost forgot why I came up here. My lunch…"

Betty smiled, poor Mr. Roi was getting old and forgetful, and not many black hairs were left on the mostly grey head.

"Came to get my lunch in the fridge," he said. "I told the other boys they could use this fridge also until we get a new one, but they didn't want to. Said they were okay, they teamed up and got a cooler with ice down by the temporary maintenance shack. I think they're just shy or something, they get all dirty and dusty mowing the fairways and don't want to come near the pro shop. Maybe they're shy about you eh?"

Betty looked at the clock on the wall. Suddenly she was the one getting old and forgetful. Lunchtime. High noon. She'd been so busy all morning checking in golfers and making sure they all got off the tee in good order that she'd forgotten about high noon and lunch, and pigs playing golf. She gritted her teeth and her left eye began to twitch.

Mr. Roi noticed the change in her demeanor. "Eh, how come you getting all humbug?" he asked. "Here, have some of my sandwich, you must be getting hungry eh?"

"No thanks Uncle Roi."

"Oh I know," said Mr. Roi, nodding his head wisely. "Those boys with Harley, they always come around noon, playing golf, wasting time eh?" He looked at her with an inquiring squint.

That brought the pidgin out of her in a flash.

"Hey whatevahs…"

Down near the first tee, three friends from Oahu were on deck and warming up, getting ready to go out for a round on the course. They'd flown over last week, and were working at a construction job nearby when they'd run out of materials and the boss gave them the day off. With nothing else to do and on a friendly neighbor island, playing a round of golf at the local course sounded like a great idea.

Sam took another practice swing, the driver whistling through the empty air. "Ho cuz, I going crank dis ball down da fairway."

"My arms are stiff from lifting all that drywall all weekend," said Blue as he massaged his bicep.

Mack was stretching his neck side to side and taking it all in. "Wow, this course is dry as a bone boys," he said. "The ball is gonna roll, no doubt about that."

"Hey check it out," said Sam. "The girl at the cashier's window, I think she's checking us out."

They all stopped what they were doing to look. It was hard to tell from this distance, plus the glare on the window. The girls' vibrant eyes were there alright, it was just hard to tell *what* they were looking at.

"I think I should ask her out on a date," said Sam.

Blue's face scrunched in surprise, and his voice went up an octave. "That local chick?" It was more of a statement than a question. "Braddah, she would chew you up and spit you out. Either that or her boyfriend will. Local chicks that look like that aren't single buddy. It's like that song, she's gotta be somebody's baby, cause she's so fine. And she is."

"Well, I gotta try man, can you believe those eyes?"

"Alright," said Blue. "Just make sure there's no one lurking in the back shadows when you pop the question or you may be the one getting popped."

Betty was watching the local guys on deck as they warmed up, and saw them all look up at once at the starter's window. Part Portuguese she could read lips, and intentions from a mile away, tell what someone was saying by their body language. They were talking about her. The one with the cap started walking up the hill, smiling. "This better be good," she thought.

"Nice place you got here," he said when he got to the window.

Small talk meant no talk. Betty frowned. "Need some tees, or a scorecard?"

"No I was just wondering..." he looked past her into the darkened pro shop, searching for the shadow of someone lurking back there like Blue told him. It was empty. "...just wondering if maybe, you know, you might want to uh, you know, uh maybe go out to dinner or something?"

Now Betty, being both proficient in Pidgin and part Portagee to boot had many, *many* options for words at her disposal. The very last thing in the world she wanted was another good for nothing lazy golfer in her life, she'd tried that already. The golfer/boyfriend wannabe smiled and waited patiently. Betty thought for a nanosecond and replied to his advances.

"Beat it." She jerked her thumb towards the tee box.

His smile faded slightly, this wasn't going quite

as well as he'd hoped. He tried for an explanation. "Why, do you have a boyfriend or something?"

That was the wrong thing to ask her.

"Get lost before I have to bull whip you," she said calmly. She'd had enough of this nonsense.

"Wh..what?..." he stammered.

"You heard me," stated Betty as she pulled a coiled rope from under the desk. The Portuguese bronco buster in her was coming out and she uncoiled the bull whip, walked out of the pro shop and cracked the whip in the air. It sounded like someone fired off an elephant gun. Everyone within earshot cringed and bent over at the sound. Betty cracked the whip again. The golfer/boyfriend wannabe stumbled as he ran for his life away from the starter's shack. He tripped on the lava rocks that lined the flower bed by the first tee, rolling and rolling on the ground and ended up at the feet of his friends who were trying not to laugh for fear of being bullwhipped by the angry girl at the top of the hill.

Sam picked himself up and dusted off the grass clippings from his clothes and hair and looked around with wild eyes, like a horse that just escaped capture.

"What'd she say?" asked Blue, hiding a chuckle.

"Funny," mumbled Sam, not a bit amused as he grabbed his clubs. "Let's tee off."

Down in the parking lot the boys were getting ready for their match. Josh popped the top off another beer and threw the old one on the growing pile in the bed of the truck. They could hear the bullwhip cracking from the clubhouse and echoing down in the canyons. "Betty's working," he said casually as he blew the froth off the beer. "Man, how you ever got out of that relationship alive I'll never know."

Harley was silent, brooding. "Yeah, that sure is some wahine," he said finally. He crumpled his beer can and threw it on the pile. "A guy makes one mistake, one tiny little mistake, and a gal can't give him another chance?"

"Tiny little mistake?" scoffed Bob.

"I think she did give you a chance," said Josh. "By not bullwhipping you on sight when she found out about all those phone numbers that you and her nephew got at the mall when she was in the ER, and unconscious."

"Yeah, well…"

"You still got those numbers?" asked Bob.

"What are you kidding me? I never even kept them in the first place. I threw them in a trash can on my way out of the mall that same day. But did she ever ask me? No. She's a hard headed tight fisted bull whipping…"

"Bitch?" asked Bob.

"Ahhh…" started Harley and then drank his beer in silence, his brow furrowing and darkening his already gloomy eyes.

Archie pulled up in his Hummer and got out slowly. He had a brace on his knee and was walking with crutches. Harley narrowed his eyes. "Oh this should be good."

It took a few minutes for Archie to get to them, having such a hard time maneuvering around the parked cars and wincing with every step.

"Beer?" asked Josh, and gave one to a sad but nodding Arch.

"Crutches huh?" asked Harley.

"Afraid so," said a glum Archie.

"Stinger?" asked Bob.

"Worse," said Archie. "I was coming down the stairs this morning…

"Those damn stairs again," said Bob, "maybe you should look into a one story house, or an elevator."

"Can I finish my story?… and I tripped…"

"Over a bag of money?" asked Josh.

"What, do you think I have bags of money lying around my house?"

"Well I would if I were in your shoes," said Josh. "I'd have a swimming pool filled with cash and just dive into it once in awhile for the heck of it."

"My cat, I stepped over…"

"Poor Mr. Whiskers?" interrupted Josh.

"I stepped over the lazy cat that was sleeping on a step, and I missed the next one. Geez Harley, what's it gonna take to get a break in this game?"

"Hey I've got an idea."

"What's that?"

"Play some better golf."

"No strokes?"

"I'll tell you what, if you're on your death bed, and the priest is giving you the last rites, I'll give you one stroke per nine."

"That's harsh."

"How about *you* give *us* strokes for being a putz?"

"Alright lighten up a little will ya? I guess I better take off this brace and loosen it up a little."

"So what's the injury?"

"Strained minushka."

"Sounds like something you eat at a Japanese restaurant."

"It's a little ligament that runs along the knee."

"You went to Dr. Malley?"

"Yeah, he told me to stay off of it for a few days."

"So what are you doing here?"

"You think a little minushka's gonna derail me? Not a chance." It was then that Archie noticed the giant blood stained bandages wrapped around Josh's legs. It looked like he came off a battlefield. "What the heck happened to you?" he asked.

"Chompers."

"Oh," said Archie, and no further explanation was necessary. "You gettin' strokes?"

Josh looked down and shook his head dejectedly, and Harley grinned on the side. "That's a good one Archie."

They walked up the hill and gathered at the back of the first tee so the starter could confirm that they were all present and accounted for and Archie walked up to the window and signed them up. The place was pretty quiet, even for a Tuesday.

"We're second up," said Archie as he pulled out his driver and did some stretching and took a couple of practice swings.

Bob elbowed Josh and nodded towards Archie. Josh looked bewildered for moment and then smiled as he remembered their plan. "Oh yeah." He pulled out his own driver and started doing his own stretching and practice swinging. "So Archie, I got a question."

"Yeah Josh."

"Does Marlena like pillow fights?"

115

"What?"

"Does she like pillow fights, you know, like at slumber parties. You always see movies of girls having pillow fights at slumber parties, and I was just wondering if she was into that sort of thing."

"Pillow fights. You're asking if my future fiancé likes pillow fights?"

"It's just a simple question, you don't have to get all defensive."

"I think you're a funny guy Josh and it's a funny question, and I really don't know the answer to it, but I'll get back to you, how's that?"

Bob stepped to the side with his own driver, took a long slow swing, and joined the conversation. "Does she have a propensity for pillows? I mean, does she seem interested in their construction? Does she count them and measure them? Does she weigh them and test their density by squeezing them and pressing them up against her face, or better yet against your face?"

"What the hell is wrong with you two guys?"

Harley was marking his golf ball with a pen and decided it was time to step in. "What if she's a money grubbing pillow smothering gold digger who's only after your money? We're not talking half the money, as in wait until you're married, then getting a quickie divorce half of the money. What if she wants the whole enchilada?"

"You think Marlena's gonna smother me with a pillow so she can take all my money? You guys are crazy."

"Hey it's just a 'what if' scenario pal, it wouldn't be the first time something like that happened. We're just looking out for you." Harley shrugged his shoulder and went back to marking golf balls. "Hey, whatever pal. It's your life."

Archie smiled and wagged his finger at them. "Oh I see what's going on. You guys are trying to rattle me on the first tee with all this talk about pillow fights and money grubbing pillow smothering ballet dancers. Woooooo, scaaaary."

"We're trying to save you," said Bob.

"I'm already lost, so don't even try. I'm asking Marlena to marry me in a couple of days, so back off."

The group ahead of them was on the green and putting and they moved up onto the tee box.

"On the tee we have the Crumper foursome. On deck Mackey threesome, third up Santos…PLEASE WAIT TILL THE GROUP AHEAD OF YOU IS PUTTING BEFORE TEEING OFF…" crackle.

Harley ignored the starter's window, snuggled his hand into the glove and teed up his ball. He wasted little time and smacked it straight and far down the middle.

"Time to take care of business boys," he said as he picked up his tee.

Archie was next up, and took his usual awkward stance, back foot behind parallel, arms over extended, hands gripping and un-gripping the club. He exhaled and thought about the DVD and the bungee cord exercises grooving his swing plane. "You got this," he said and brought the club sloooowly back to the top of the arc, then rotated his inner core back and through, bringing his arms down with the rotation and smashing the clubface straight through the ball and watched as it went perfectly down the middle of the fairway and then curved to the right slicing towards the out of bounds markers.

"Arrrghhhh," he yelled, while his group shouted heartily for the ball to go out of bounds, and then sighing as it hit the palm tree and bounced back to the fairway.

"I planned that," said Archie as he retrieved his tee.

While Josh was setting up and eyeing up his projected path down the fairway with his ball on the tee, Archie cleared his throat. "Let's meet up at the Swamp tonight, my treat."

The Swamp was a new restaurant in town, which was trying to copy the success of the Cave and the Pit. Some rumors running around the town were that they served bootleg whiskey and road kill, and the waitresses were the meanest on the planet.

Josh was unmoved by the offer and proceeded to hit his drive nice and easy down the middle. He picked up his tee and pointed at Archie. "That's dirty pool offering free food when a hungry guy is getting ready to hit."

Bob hit his normal low and dirty runner down the middle and they were off and running.

Archie nuzzled his second shot ten feet from the hole and knocked it in for a birdie and the early lead while the competition expressed their displeasure.

"Early ripe, early rotten," said Bob.

"Or so we hope," chimed Josh.

On the second hole Archie absolutely bombed the longest drive he'd ever hit and it soared well over the hill. "Damn," he shouted as the group whistled in appreciation. Maybe that ballet stuff was working after all he thought, he'd taken his first private lesson from Marlena this morning, and he could really feel the difference in his balance. The other guys hit their second shots before they could even see Archie's ball, and when they got over the hill, there it was, halfway down the fairway with an easy wedge to the green, he could be there in two and be putting for eagle, oh yeah. He whistled a little tune as he walked down the hill towards his ball. It even looked like it was sitting up a bit, almost like it was teed up on the grass, and as he got closer he saw why, and his heart sank as he looked down at it.

"I need a ruling!" he shouted at the other guys who were sitting in their carts on the side. Harley was first on the scene and he waved the other guys over, and they all shook their heads in dismay.

"Darn shame," said Josh.

"Tough break," winced Bob.

"You know the rules," said Harley. "Play it as it lies."

Problem was, where it lied was right on top of a giant fresh pile of doggy doo-doo. Archie looked around and saw the culprit bouncing along with his tail high a couple of fairways over. It was a huge dog, probably a mastiff or a golden retriever. "Hey you!" he shouted at the dog but the mongrel kept on its way without looking back. "I've seen that dog before; it lives over on that house at the bottom of the seventh fairway."

"Its Jenkins dog," said Bob. "He keeps it fenced in, must have gotten loose."

"He got loose in more ways than one," said Josh. "Wow, what the heck does he feed that dog, elephant food?"

"Well Jenkins owes me a golf ball," said Archie as he reached in his golf bag for a new ball and got ready to drop it.

"What do you think you're doing?" asked Harley.

"Dropping a ball, what does it look like?"

"You know the rules buddy, play it where it lies."

"From that? You're crazy. It's a man made obstruction. The royal and ancient rules of golf clearly state that a ball resting upon a man made obstruction may be moved without penalty, and if said golf ball has been damaged by the object, then a new ball may be put in play. I quote."

"How in the heck is that a manmade object?"

"Bob just said it was Jenkins' dog right? It's obviously not a wild dog running around and hunting caribou like a wolf in Alaska. It's a domesticated animal that has been bred by mankind over the millennium, this particular canine systematically hand fed by a man who we all know by name, and fed quite well by the looks of it, and therefore that disgusting obstruction that my ball is currently resting upon is in fact man made. I rest my case."

The group behind them whistled and gave an angry wave, wishing them to hit the ball already. They were obviously tourists and the group ignored them and went back to their discussion.

"You're forgetting the turkey ruling," said Harley, and Archie winced.

A few years back right around Thanksgiving the turkey incident happened upon which the aforementioned turkey ruling was based. Archie had somehow conveniently forgotten about it.

Old man Teves owned a farm nearby and bred turkeys throughout the year which he sold the week before Thanksgiving and used the proceeds to pay the mortgage on his land. One of the turkeys, a prize hen weighing over twenty five pounds had escaped the butchers block and made its way onto the golf course during their match. It was hiding in the bushes along the third fairway looking for grubs and whatnot when Harley hit a low running drive along the edge where the bird was busily scratching the ground. It saw the ball rolling nearby and thinking it was a strange kind of bug, ran out onto the fairway, gobbled it up and immediately choked to death on it.

When they got to the bird it lay there with the ball still visible in the gullet, and Harley began to reach down to retrieve it but Archie and the gang stopped him, and after the same kind of argument they were having now, decided that Harley would either play the ball where it lay, or take a one stroke penalty for an unplayable lie. Harley decided to try his luck and hit the ball out of the turkeys' mouth and onto the green. Incredible bad timing had the farmer come over the hill and at the very moment of impact witness his prize turkey being mutilated by Harley and chased him around the course with a pitchfork. Harley lost the hole and the match for leaving the course, and the turkey ruling became local legend. No one ever found out what happened to the turkey. For all anyone knew, Jenkins dog dragged it off.

"Ah yes, the turkey ruling," said Archie as he analyzed the situation. "This is a bit of a pickle," he murmured, and he imagined how it would unfold if he did in fact try to hit the ball out of the pile and he grimaced and quickly dropped a new ball a few paces to the side. "I'll take the penalty."

Harley and Josh tied with birdies, and it was a

carryover to the third hole which Archie won with a bogey. And just like that he was up three holes to none.

Golf is a game of opposites. You hit down on the ball to make it go up, you hit on the right side of it to make it go left, the left side of it to make it go right, and so on. When a golfer sets up to hit a shot especially with an iron, there's a certain uneasiness that creeps into his sub consciousness. The iron and ball are at odds with each other, consisting of diametrically opposed compositions, the ball perfectly round with dimples on the surface to cut the air flow, inner core of rubber, outer core of balata or plastic of some sort, no one really knew what it was made of for sure and if you asked them they would fumble with some words and then quickly change the subject, but the iron was made of, well, iron, man stuff, steel hardened and forged in the same kind of mill where they made beams for skyscrapers, and engine blocks for race cars.

There's a certain sort of sound and feel for a golfer when he hits a ball with his club perfectly flush, right in the center of the clubface, it almost feels like you just hit a bouncy super ball or a ball consisting of a mixture of jelly and warm butter, you don't even really feel the ball hit the club since it's such a smooth and precise hit, the metal clubface and shaft and rubber grip absorbing all the impact in perfect harmony, sort of like a harmonic conversion, and it has that smooth unmistakable whoosh sound; a sound that for a golfer is like hearing a symphony, it's kind of like a whoosh sound mixed with warm butter and goodness.

That's not the sound that they all heard when

Harley hit the ball off the fourth tee. It sounded more like 'clank'. To Harley it felt like he just hit a boulder the size of a car with his club and the boulder didn't move. The shock reverberated up from the club through his hands wrist and arms while the ball went straight down into the valley, out of bounds and out of the running for the hole.

The rest of them hit safely over the gulley, but none were able to hold the green and the balls rolled off one side and the other, but now they had it surrounded, and headed around the corner.

Josh lined up for the shot. He was fifty feet off the green and he had a Texas wedge in his hand, a putter. The ground in front of the green was so packed and hard that it was impossible to get a wedge under the ball, and so putting was usually called for. Archie however scoffed at this method. Josh gave the ball a good smack and it rolled down the fairway, onto the green and curved toward the hole ending up twenty feet from the pin. A respectable effort he thought.

"Nice shot Nancy," said Bob from the side. "Does your husband play too?"

A fusillade of swearing flowed towards Bob who lined up his shot which was just off the green.

Sure, he could have putted the ball but he watched the golf channel every day and seeing those pros chip from off the green convinced him that he could do the same. Plus, he reasoned, if he kept working at it he would get better at the chipping game, while the other guys, the 'putties' as he referred to them would be stuck with that shot and never be able to play very well at a real golf course. He swung the club ever so gently intending to clip the ball just underneath it and have it pop onto the fringe of the green and roll ever so slowly into the cup. The ground, being the consistency of asphalt bounced the club face up on top of the ball which then shot forward like a bullet past the cup and nearly off the green followed by a stream of profanity that would make a prison guard blush.

Bob and Josh ended up tying on the hole, one tie all tie, much to the delight of Archie and Harley who pointed at each other like gunfighters at the OK corral. It was on to the fifth hole with Archie still up by three and two dots on the line.

On the fifth hole, a short par four, Bob and Archie hit out of bounds on their tee shots and were out of it. Harley hit his second shot onto the green and a mere twenty feet from the pin, while Josh's second shot hit the cart path and bounced way past the green and was nestled in the rough about a hundred feet away, almost by the next tee.

"Finally!" yelled Harley. "Finally I get some breathing room." No way was Josh going to get up and down from that spot in two for his par. Hell, he might have a tough time getting in the hole in three for a bogey from where he was. All I need to do now, thought Harley about his own shot, is nuzzle my putt up next to the hole and tap in for par to win the carry over holes

Josh got to his ball and pulled out his putter and went through his whole routine, kicking off his shoes, adjusting his hat, lining up the putt, taking some practice swings. Josh wasn't the best putter on the island, but he was definitely one of the luckiest. He was known to knock in fifty footers from off the green to win all the marbles.

"A lot of it is just believing it's going to go in,"

he'd say.

Harley was getting impatient and wanted to get going with winning the hole. "While we're young!" he yelled, and everyone laughed. Josh ignored them and continued with his pre-shot routine.

At the scenic pavilion that was situated way out on the point, a wedding party was in full swing. One of the guests had left the party and was in a fine mood, hitting golf balls from the next tee over the ravine. A cowboy lean and strong, he was dressed in blue jeans and boots, button down shirt and ten gallon hat and stood on the tee trying to hit the ball over the ravine without falling over backwards. He spotted Josh nearby and shouted out to him.

"Eh dare Josh! Ow you bin!" The cowboy was sloshed.

Harley frowned from the green, and muttered. "C'mon Josh, just hit the damn shot."

The drunken cowboy sauntered over and shook Josh's hand, and gave him a big drunken hug.

"Hair you go my fren," he bellowed. "I gift you my brannew golf club."

"That's okay," smiled Josh as he admired the club. "Sure is a nice one, but I've already got a five wood in my bag."

"Yo shure yo dohn wanna havit?"

"Nope, but thanks for the offer."

The cowboy was taken aback. "Bran-new."

"No thanks."

The cowboy stood straight with a stern face and ramrod back. It looked like he was gonna clobber Josh for the refusing the club. And then he smiled and bellowed anew.

"You awright Josh." And as the cowboy walked back to the tee by the ravine he shouted back to Josh while pointing his finger directly at him. "You gonna have good luck all day my frien!"

Harley looked at the other players. "He didn't just say that did he? Good luck? Did he just say good luck? You can't wish a golfer good luck when he's in a match with someone. What the hell is wrong with that damn cowboy?"

And so with the good wishes of the drunken cowboy hanging over his head like a golden halo, Josh stood over the ball and whacked it a good one with the putter. They all stood in silence as it rolled up and over the hill, onto the green, rolling and rolling until it bounced against the flagstick and straight down into the hole for a birdie three.

Josh yelped with glee and danced a jig all the way to the cup while a loud mix of anguish and pain emanated from the others. And now forced to make a twenty foot birdie putt to tie, Harley missed by a mile, and Josh won the hole and the carryover.

Archie had three dots, Josh had two, and Bob and Harley were getting shut out. There were four holes to go.

They tied again on the sixth hole, and it was a carryover to the seventh.

Harley decided it was time to make his move.

The seventh tee is at the bottom of the hill and Harley being the crazed dragster that he was, liked to race to the bottom, crank the wheel and slam on the brakes, skidding the cart sideways on the gravel for fun. Archie was usually the passenger and had to either lean left or be ready to leap out at a moment's notice if the cart flipped over.

This time he wasn't so lucky.

Bob and Josh came around the corner of the

hedge and could see down the fairway to the tee at the bottom of the hill. The other cart was flipped over on its side and Harley was struggling to lift it. Archie was nowhere in sight. They realized that Archie was UNDER the cart.

"He's dead," muttered Bob. "Holy cow, he killed Archie!"

By the time they got to the stricken cart, Harley had succeeded in lifting it upright and Archie crawled out from under it, limping and brushing himself off. His knees and hands where they'd met the gravel, were bloodied and torn.

They all looked him over and quickly determined that he was for the most part alright and no bones were broken.

"Well, that's one way to end his win streak," said Bob. "Flip the cart on him."

Everyone laughed except Archie who looked shaken. "What the hell is wrong with you Harley?"

"Hey, it's not my fault, the tires hit a rut. This course is really going downhill. No pun intended."

Archie showed him his bloody left palm. "This is worth at least a stroke for this hole, at least until the bleeding stops, c'mon now."

Harley threw him a dirty towel from the cart. "Stop your crying, it's just a little road rash."

"Strokes Harley."

"None. You're the guy beating up on us, we're the ones who should be getting the strokes."

Bob and Josh thought about this excellent analysis, and turned to Archie for an answer.

"Yeah," Bob said. "Don't be a wuss. You're up with three dots, we should get at least a stroke on this hole, the way you've been hitting it."

Archie shook his head with disgust, mopped his

hands dry with the muddy towel, and pulled out his driver. "Alright, I'll show you guys."

"Atta way to get a spine," said Harley, as he grinned inside. They were playing Archie like a fiddle, and had him just where they wanted him, overconfident and mad as hell, and sure enough Archie tried to hit the cover off the ball to really show them who was boss, but instead hit a pop fly that barely made it past the red tees.

"Tough break," said Harley, teeing it up and hitting a little shot safe and down the middle to lull the others into doing the same.

The seventh fairway borders a grass filled pasture lined with towering fragrant eucalyptus trees. The minty flavored scent in the air was known to fill one and all with a sense of goodness and right, and if you stood quiet at the tee box for a moment you could hear the faint buzzing of thousands of honey bees in the distance, they seemed to be attracted to the eucalyptus flowers and there was always a few bee hives in the gentle swaying tree limbs nearby. You could hear them, but you couldn't see them in the nearby forest. On a clear day you could see the jungle shrouded mountains rising in the north and the east, and the coastline stretching and rounding out to the south, gentle waves breaking along the shoreline while a brisk trade wind drives steady whitecaps on the horizon. It's a peaceful setting that brings calm and gentle thoughts to all who partake of it.

In the grass filled pasture stood a large brown animal, its head down and buried in the grass, oblivious to all around it, grazing serenely on the fresh greenery.

"Hey check it out," said Bob. "A horse."

They all stopped what they were doing and looked over at it.

Josh snorted. "That's not a horse, it's a mule."

"How can you tell?" asked Bob.

"By the tail, it's kind of short, and bushy. You see a mule is a cross between a horse and a donkey, and that animal has a little bit of the characteristics of both."

"That's not a mule," stated Archie matter of factly. "That's a pure bred donkey, no doubt about it, and I can prove it."

"Oh yeah, how's that?"

Archie winked. "Watch." And he cupped his hands by his mouth, took a deep breath, and shouted at the top of his lungs. "Haarleeey, yee haw, ee haw, ee-hawww, Harley!" The sound of his ee-hawing echoed through the valleys, but the animal did not budge, and kept its head down in the grass, busy at work.

Harley shook his head and frowned, sorely disappointed with the spectacle. "You guys are pathetic," he said. "That's neither a horse, nor a mule, nor a donkey."

"Oh yeah, so what is it then?" asked Josh. "Mr. know-it-all."

"It's a jackass, and I can prove it. Watch." And he put his two small fingers at the corners of his mouth and whistled a quick ear shattering blast, and shouted, "Archie!" The animal lifted his head; his ears prickled straight up and looked directly at them on the tee while Harley nodded sagely. "See?"

Archie lost the last four holes and the match, and watched glumly as Harley danced in the parking lot with a single quarter held high. For some reason the shrill whistle and seeing the donkey look up when his name was called had a negative effect on his golf swing. Or it could have been the other guys hee-hawing all the way up the fairways, and on the greens while he was lining up his putts.

8.

The Little Miss Aloha Dance Studio was in full swing on a Tuesday afternoon. The littlest of the ballerinas, the 'under ten' crew were finishing up their after school classes, while the middle school hip hop company was about to start hipping and hopping. The parking lot was full of parents who were either there to pick up their toddlers from ballet, or dropping off their daughters for hip hop, some doing double duty, picking up one set and dropping off another. Dance instruction was big business on the island. For some reason unknown to man, women loved to dance, it was mystery that none could fathom, and none really cared to try.

Nearby, a middle aged Grandpa, a little gray around the edges and recently retired, was parking his car with his Granddaughter in the passenger seat. A jokester at heart, he turned to her and said with mirth in his eyes.

"Hey, I've got a great idea, what do you say you skip dance today, and we'll go do something fun instead?"

The little girl looked at him with fear and astonishment. "Oh no Grandpa, I really like dancing." Her hand was on the door knob, suddenly afraid that the old man was serious. How could someone joke about something like this? More fun than dancing?

He winked at her. "Well, okay you run along now, I'll pick you up in about an hour." And he chuckled as she hurried off to the dance school. "Women."

The ballet room now vacant of the little ones, was occupied by our heroines. The music played soft classical music, and the women ranging in age from twenty to thirty and more were stretching and getting ready for their class. Zumba was all the rage, and while the girls did partake in that jungle dance most days of the week, Tuesday was ballet night. It kept them calm and focused and balanced, and well, classy.

"And one, and two, and three, and rest," whispered Angie as she leaned against the balance bar and dipped and plied (Plee – aid). "And one and two and three and rest." She turned to the woman next to her who was also balancing on the bar and dipping and resting. "So how was work today?"

"Fine, just fine," said Betty. "And one and two and three... The pigs were there, ...and two and three... played two rounds... and rest. Lucky for me that Archie checked them in, I didn't have to talk to the others."

"Maybe it wouldn't be so bad," said Melissa on the other side of Betty, in between dipping and resting. "Archie and Marlena can have their lives and we can have ours, and we don't really need to mingle with the pigs. We've gotten along fine so far, it hasn't been so bad."

The other two looked at her and frowned.

"I almost barfed when I saw that the 'friends' that Marlena had invited to the Cave last night turned out to be the pigs," said Betty. "And one, and two, and three, and rest. I had to go home and work on the punching bag after we left. And one and two..."

"I know," said Angie. "I thought it was going to

be some of the cute guys that have been hitting on her lately, and some of their friends."

"Like Zach, or Randall," said Betty.

"Or George, or Lawrence," said Melissa. "What the heck is wrong with her? And two, and three…"

"As long as I don't get dragged into it I don't care," said Betty. "I have to see the swine every day at the course, that's enough for me. And one and two."

The smooth and soothing Beethoven waltz was interrupted by a sound like fabric tearing.

Melissa scrunched her face. "Did you just fart?"

"It came from over there," said Betty, pointing to Angie.

Angie's face turned beet red. "It wasn't me," she protested.

"Whoever denied it supplied it," said Betty.

"Gross," said Melissa. "One, and two, and three, and rest."

Marlena swept into the room, graceful as ever. "Girls, girls, girls," she half sang. "How are we all doing today, are we ready to practice our number? The winter recital is just around the corner."

"We're all doing fine, but Angie over here had too many burritos last night," said Betty.

Marlena did a pirouette over to the side and turned up the air conditioner. "Problem solved," she said, and began stretching on the bar. "My first dance instructor was very strict, she said we should all get our talking done while stretching, and that way we can focus on the dance and nothing else."

"You're a little bubbly today," said Angie. "Been nipping at the Sake in the back?"

"Of course not," laughed Marlena. "It's just so

much fun teaching ballet to the children; they're so little and cute, and have so much fun being little ballerinas. Plus I had a wonderful night at the Cave last night."

"You did?" asked Melissa.

"Why?" asked Betty.

"Why?" asked Marlena. "Well Archie is just so much fun to be around. We danced we ate, we sang..."

"Oh yeah, the singing, now I remember," said Betty and she winced. "You really shouldn't do that in public."

"You girls seemed to have a bit of fun also, if you'd admit it to yourselves," said Marlena.

"Now I'm sure you've been hitting the bottle," said Betty.

"Look," said Angie. "We wanted to talk to you about Archie before you got any more serious with him."

"Oh?"

"Well," said Melissa. "He's sort of known around town, if you know what I mean..."

"Look," said Betty. "Let's not dance around the subject as it were. Archie's a playboy. He has lots of money, and has had lots of girls. In fact we don't even know how many, no one really does, even his friends. For all we know he could have a girlfriend on every continent."

Marlena's face went blank. She was in shock, her mouth was open and round and she brought her hand up to cover it. Her eyes were wide with fear. "Not my Archie..."

The girls all nodded sympathetically, and then Marlena laughed and laughed. "You girls are funny.

You see, in my country it is very bad luck to even think about getting serious with a boy who has not how do you say, 'played the field', because you don't want them to settle down with you and one day to think to themselves that they never played the field and missed out on something, you want them to settle down *after* they played the field, understand?"

Melissa frowned. "What kind of luck is it when you settle down with a guy who played the field before they settled down, and keeps doing it after."

"We've heard from Melissa and Angie why they broke up with their significant others..." started Marlena.

Angie had a look of disgust on her face. "Significant others?"

"..what I'm curious is what caused you and Harley to split up Betty. You seem to have a sort of banter, a repertoire together."

Betty kept stretching. "Repertoire? Is that what you call it?"

"There's a spark, I can see it."

"That's not a spark, that's a volcanic eruption," said Angie. "Don't get too close to it."

"So what's the story?" asked Marlena.

Angie shook her head. "I warned her..."

"You want to know the story? I'll tell you the story. You see this scar?" Betty showed Marlena a line on the side of her knee.

"Oh my God he hit you."

"No he didn't hit me. He wouldn't dare, I'd knock him the hell out. You see I had this nagging injury when I took a tumble in a rodeo, a torn anterior cruciate ligament. I decided to have it surgically repaired, and the best guy is on Oahu, so I ask Harley if he'd like to go over there with me, we can have a little vacation in Waikiki, see my sister and her family who live there, and I can get the surgery done the right way, okay?"

"Okay."

"Anyways, they put me under for the surgery and it takes about an hour, plus a couple of hours in the recovery room. Harley gets bored and takes my eight year old nephew who is at the hospital, to the mall nearby to pick up chicks."

"What? Oh,oh."

"Yeah, my nephew tells me all about it when I'm waking up in the recovery room. I'm all groggy and in a fog, and he was so proud of himself. 'We asked ten of the prettiest girls we could find Auntie', he says. 'And we got five phone numbers', he tells me. 'Three said they had boyfriends, and two said they weren't interested, but we got five numbers. That's a fifty percent success ratio Auntie', he says. 'It's good to bring along a little kid Auntie, it helps break the ice', he tells me."

"How do you like that? I'm in the hospital unconscious under the knife, and good 'ol Harley is out picking up girls. When he came in the room and saw my face he must have known that I knew. 'I was teaching him a life lesson', Harley tells me. 'He'll need to know how to pick up chicks when he gets older', he says, 'it'll help his self confidence'. And then he turned to my nephew and whispers to him, 'you forgot the first lesson I told you, what happens with the guys, stays with the guys'. 'I wasn't going to keep the numbers honey', he tries telling me, 'it was all for fun', he says, 'it was all for the boy'. Yeah right. Good 'ol Harley. I'd probably be in labor having his baby and he'd be at a strip club collecting numbers."

"Did you ever think he might have been telling the truth?" asked Marlena.

"Nope."

"Couldn't give him the benefit of the doubt?"

"Not a chance, that's the last time I was within ten feet of him until last night. I told him if I ever got close enough I'd break his face. I must be getting soft. And one and two and three, and rest..."

"Well, I'm not so sure about you three girls," said Marlena, as she took her foot off the bar and replaced it with other one. "You all seem to have jumped to conclusions. You Angie caught Josh with another girl, but as he says he was just asleep and had no idea the other girl was even there. You Melissa hear gossip from a known tramp and take it like it's the gospel truth, and you Betty hear testimony from your very own nephew and use it against poor Harley. I think you should all give them another chance, I really do."

The looks on the three ranged from astonishment to outright hostility.

"In fact," continued Marlena. "I'll bet you all would very much like to get back together with those three guys, and if you did, we could all have a wonderful time. I can see it now, Archie and his best friends, and me and my best friends. It makes perfect sense. I'm just saying." She took her foot off the bar and pirouetted to the door and smiled at them. "I'm going to get a sip of water and then we can begin."

"She's gone insane," said Angie as she disappeared around the corner.

"Bonkers," said Melissa.

"Those two," said Betty, seething between her

teeth. "Are going down."

Marlena passed by the reception area and the owner of the dance studio flagged her down. "You have a phone call sweetie, line one, I was just about to track you down."

Marlena frowned, suddenly worried. "I wonder who it could be."

The voice on the other end was deep and scratchy and sounded a little edgy. "Young lady…"

She sighed in relief as she recognized her father's voice. "Hi Poppa. I was going to call you later tonight."

"Marlena, baby daughter, how are you doing, we are so worried about you."

"Don't be Poppa, everything is fine, I'm fine."

"You are so far away, in a strange country."

"It's nice here, all the people are all nice. I have new friends, a good job."

"A job? Marlena…"

"Now Poppa, you know I love to dance ballet and I also love to teach."

"But Marlena, a job?"

"I love to work Poppa, I love to make my own money."

"This is nonsense, you know that. You can teach ballet here in your own hometown. Not as a job, but as a hobby, to give back to the community."

"Please understand…"

"We worry about you, I worry about you as always for other reasons. As any father would. Does anyone know about you besides being a ballet teacher? Do they know about us, your family?"

"No Poppa, as far as anyone knows I am just Marlena the ballet instructor from Brazil. And that's how I'm going to keep it."

"We should send your bodyguards to watch over you. They can be discreet, no one needs to know they are even there. They can just be nearby, just in case of trouble."

"Poppa there will be no trouble. Please let me have this time to myself for awhile. I promise I'll call you every day."

"You are just like your mother you know, impetuous and…"

"I know, I love you too Daddy."

"Two months Marlena, as promised, to find yourself."

"Thank you Daddy, and don't worry, I'll call you tomorrow."

He said goodnight and she hung up the phone and sighed, and then scrunched her face in concern. So what if they were one of the richest families in all of Brazil? Nobody here would care about that even if they did know. Movies stars could come and go here and no one paid them the slightest homage, it seemed that what was more important here was who caught the biggest fish, or whose child was doing great in school or sports. Being rich or famous was almost laughed at here, as if it was a drawback to the good life. She was tired of all the pomp and circumstance back home, the daughter of a mining magnate, she was more of an object than a person of inner worth. She just wanted to live a simple life. Sure Archie was borderline poor, but she didn't care about that one little bit. He tried hard, and she could tell he had a good heart.

Just look at the friends he has, she told herself. Why, they are like the salt of the earth, the type of characters that you read about in books, all scruffy and loud and boisterous, and maybe a little dirty around the ears, but they were dirty on the outside, not the other way around. She loved being part of their little group, it was more real and true than what she had back home, everyone groveling at her family's feet for money... it was disgusting.

She could spot a well dressed snake a mile away after growing up around the money and power that surrounded her family. Her new friends were more genuine than that. Sure they fought a lot, that much was obvious, but that is what real people do when they have problems, they were honest about it and talked about it, they didn't hide their emotions and intentions for ulterior motives.

"If it's the last thing I do," she told herself, as she marched back into the ballet room, "I'll bring them all back together again."

9.

WEDNESDAY

Dawn at the stables comes slowly, and for a long time it's only a dull and ghostly glow somewhere over the eastern horizon, no color or form, more of a feeling than something you can actually see, just a slight difference to the black of the night that is fading off to the west. You can hear the waves crashing against the cliffs nearby and rushing up the beach far down on the coast, the horses breathing steadily in the darkness, and the roosters crowing in the distance are the only other sounds on an otherwise quiet morning.

Betty had been at work since four AM, as usual she was the first one there, cleaning the stables and feeding the hungry horses, who were also early risers, and like her, their eyes gleamed bright and alive with the new day. There were thirty five horses in all, workers, strong and big and ready to carry the tourists that would soon arrive by the dozens to ride the trails along the coast.

The owner of the stables walked out of the office carrying two cups of steaming coffee in big ceramic mugs and made his way towards the corral where Betty was pouring the last of the oat pellets into the plastic bins in the corral. He was a grizzled old cowboy in his late sixties but still had plenty of black hair and a gnarled glint in his eye that would make the young toughs look away quickly and the ladies give a second glance. When he was a young man he won the World Bull riding Championships and he still looked like he had a streak of wildness in him, and he had that slight bowlegged walk that told you he'd been riding on a horse most of his life.

"Take a break Betty," he said, "and join me for a cuppa java, wontcha?.

She wrapped up the empty bag of feed, tossing it in a nearby trashcan and reached for the coffee. "Why thank you Orly." She sipped at the coffee and sighed. "It's good."

They leaned against the wood picket fence and watched the horses munching on the feed as the sky begin to color at the horizon with deep reds and orange while sipping on the hot brew.

"Betty, how long have you been working here?"

She was puzzled. "You mean today?"

He laughed. "No, I mean how many years. Do you remember when you first started working for me?"

She hadn't expected the question and shook her head. "I don't know, it seems like both forever, and yesterday at the same time. Why do you ask?"

"Because I remember as clear as a bell the day you came to me and asked for a job. It was exactly fifteen years ago today, I have it written on the calendar in the office. Fifteen years ago to this very day you rode your little bike in here and marched right up to me and asked if you could work here, said you'd take any job I could give you. You were all of eleven years old, four foot high and about eighty pounds full of piss and vinegar, and I laughed out loud, but then I saw how serious you were and saw the tears at the edges of your eyes, and I gave you a job cleaning out the stables that very afternoon. I had you sweeping out the horse turds and cleaning the floors, the most disgusting jobs that I could think of just to get rid of you. I paid you three dollars cash for three hours of butt busting work and I thought that's the last I'd seen of you. But I'll be dolgurned if you didn't come back the very next day, and the day after that, and every day since. I've gone through dozens of so called tough cow hands who quit because they couldn't handle the hard work and yet here you are."

"I like the work, and I like the money."

"I've got to say you are about the most stubborn person whether man or woman or animal that I have ever met."

"Why thank you Orly, that's about the nicest thing I've heard today." She remembered the first day she worked here alright, not like it was yesterday but like it was a few minutes ago. Her Dad had just lost his job at the sugar mill along with everyone else that had been laid off when the sugar industry went belly up, put out of business by cheap labor and land in Asia. All the mills on the island slowly but surely shut their doors and with so many people out of work, there just wasn't enough to go around, and her Dad being one of the older workers had the toughest time of it. Planting and harvesting sugar was all he knew, and pretty soon the unpaid bills began piling up and they were in danger of losing the house and the car and everything else. Sometimes there wasn't enough food to eat, and they went hungry. She remembered seeing her Mom crying one night at the kitchen table, which was bad enough, but when she saw her good old Dad by the back of the garage after coming home from another day of finding no work and she saw the tears he was hiding in the corners of his eyes, it was too much for a little girl to bear and she got on her bike and rode as fast as she could to the horse ranch. Oh yeah, she remembered that day alright. She took that three dollars and hid it in her Dad's pants pockets, and every time she got paid after that she put it safely in a little box that she hid in her closest, and at the end of the month she handed her Dad a hundred dollars and saved the day. She would never, ever give up this job, no way. More than anything it reminded her of those tough days that she never wanted to forget.

"So seeing that it's a milestone in a way, your fifteen year anniversary working at the stables and all; and by the way Betty, fifteen has always been a good luck number for me. It took me fifteen bulls before I figured out how to ride one to the end of the bell, I won fifteen thousand dollars for the Bull riding Championship which I used to buy this little horse ranch, and I just got back yesterday from Las Vegas where I put a hundred dollars on the number fifteen and won fifteen hundred dollars."

"Wow! Congratulations, that's awesome."

"And since it's been a lucky fifteen years of having you as my most trustworthy employee I am gifting you a bonus of fifteen dollars." He handed her a small wad of singles.

She looked at it and frowned. "For a minute there I thought you were going to hand me fifteen hundred dollars."

He laughed a belly roll and slapped his thigh. "Ha ha, yeah well I lost those winnings about a minute later when I put it all on the number fifteen again." He shook his head and sighed. "Vegas always wins."

She took the money and stuffed it in her jeans front pocket, a bonus was a bonus. "How many riders do you have today Orly?"

"Ten so far."

She was disappointed again. "I thought you were going to say fifteen."

"I'm hoping for twenty or thirty but it's shaping up to be a slow day, maybe some more tourists will call from the hotels later in the morning. Let's saddle up ten to start with, and see where she goes."

They got busy saddling up the horses while they were all busy feeding, and by the time the sun had cleared the horizon, ten were ready to ride.

Betty pulled the belly belt on the last horse, cinching it tight; checking the top to make sure it was solid and the patted the horse on the haunches.

"That's ten Orly. Check it out, the other horses are looking sad, like they're getting left out of an adventure."

"Yeah, well they'll get their turn, good work Betty. Are you up at the golf course today?"

"Ten o'clock sharp."

He spit on the ground and finished cinching up his horses' saddle. "What a sissy sport that is, riding around in a golf cart and hitting a little ball. Pasty white pansy sport. You still like working up there?"

She shrugged. "It's a job."

"You know Betty, I remind you about this once in a while yes I do, if you ever wanted to work full time down here at the stables, I could use you from sunup to sundown, seven days a week. I'd pay you good, too."

She hesitated, as always, when he told her that; of course it would be the best job in the world, are you kidding me she thought, to work at the stables all day, to be outside running the horses, but she could never bring herself to do it, as much as she wanted, to work one job even this one, and put all of her marbles into one little basket, because if that basket ever turned upside down, like what happened to her Dad, then she'd have nothing. It was best to spread things out, and that's why she had three jobs, because you always had to have something to fall back on. She never, ever wanted to be broke again.

"Thanks Orly."

The sun was two hands over the horizon when a big blue pickup truck pulled into the dirt lot next to the barn. The young cowboy in the passenger's seat kissed the girl that was driving on the lips and the baby in the car seat on the top of the head then hopped out.

"Sorry I'm late Mr. Orly," he yelled out. "Maddie was up all night crying and my alarm didn't go off." He hustled towards the barn to saddle up his horse, and Orly saw the look on Betty's face as she watched the young family, even though she tried to hide it, there it was, regret. It was a shame, he thought, to see such a pretty young girl unmarried. He knew all about Harley, hell the whole town knew about the two of them.

"Life's a funny thing sometimes Betty. You know you can get locked onto something if you really want it enough. Kinda like riding a bull in the ring. He's a mean and ornery two thousand pounds of hoof stomping horn gouging animal and here you are on his back all of sudden, and then they wrench his nut sack to drive him a little more crazy and then open the gate, and all hell breaks loose of buckin' and slammin', but if you get your hand tucked tight enough in the binding and don't wilt, you can ride him for a bit and jump off on your own terms afore you get stomped on, or worse."

"What's your point Orly?" The old cowboy talked in riddles sometimes, but she had a feeling she knew where this was headed.

"You see that bronco over there?"

"Yeah."

A separate corral held a single brown stallion with a splash of white on his front shoulder. He was a big horse with rippling muscles and wild eyes. He would race around the corral a couple of times and then rear back on his hind legs and whinny loudly, snort a few times, stomp his front legs, then gallop over to the fence to look at them with anger flashing in his eyes, and then do all over again.

"I picked him up on auction over on the Big Island last month, had him shipped over, and just picked him up from the docks yesterday. He's a fine animal, but wild as hell. Plenty of tough cowboys tried to break him over there. Finally they all gave up and sold him rather than put a bullet in him."

"I'm glad for that."

"Anyways, I can break him, no doubt in my mind at all, but I like looking at him like he is, all wild and untamed just as nature intended, kind of like some people in a way if you know what I'm saying. Oh, I'll break him someday, but for now he's on his own. I sure do like seeing a wild horse once in a while; we don't get too many of them these days."

"Please don't tell me there's some kind of moral

hidden in that story."

"Moral? Naww, there's no moral. But just remember this Betty, when you break a horse, you can't 'un-break' it."

10.

Bob sat back in his chair and watched the long line of people filing through the metal detector at the airport. Every now and then it would beep and he'd have to ask the person who set it off to step back, have them double check their pockets, ask if they had any metal plates in their bodies, and such. It was a boring job, but every now and then it got exciting, like the time the Mayor came through, setting off the alarm over and over again. He was in a hurry, off to catch an important flight to the capital in Honolulu, whining loudly so everyone within earshot could hear, 'can't you just let me bypass the metal detector so I can get on the plane, I'm on important Government business' etc.

Unfortunately for the Mayor, Bob had lost every hole in the previous day's golf match, swept for the second time that week, and not only that, but he was forced to watch his ex girlfriend direct traffic on the other side of the road and he was in no mood to get pushed around by some low life.

"Sorry Mayor," Bob had said, "we have to follow the rules."

The Mayor looked at his watch and heard the intercom call out that his flight was ready for departure. He got into Bob's face and spoke slowly and methodically, elucidating each syllable like he was talking to a small child.

"I'm the Mayor of this County, and I need to get on that plane immediately."

"Sorry Mayor, this is Federal jurisdiction, if you would please just step over to the.."

The Mayor wasn't used to the word 'no', and being six foot five and three hundred fifty pounds reached out and pushed Bob out of the way. "I don't have time for this."

Wrong move. Not only had Bob worked most of his life mowing and trimming lawns before he got this job, he'd also studied Jujitsu since he was five. He had the Mayor pinned and cuffed in a heartbeat, and when the dust cleared they found a gram of meth on the Mayor and he went to prison. Good times.

Today though was just plain old boring, no foreigners with inadequate ID, no metal plate implants, no angry and running late VIP's needing additional screening, just him and his chair and his 'ex' girlfriend Angie directing traffic on the other side of the entry road. Lucky for him that his morning shift was almost done and he looked at his watch for the fifth time that minute.

There was a new guy on the point as they called it, they always had the new guy checking ID's at the front, flashing his infrared flashlight on the cards to see if they were fake, looking at the sides to see if they falsely laminated or printed, the usual. He had clean white teeth when he smiled which was all the time and a perfect haircut, not a follicle out of place, buff and trim in his ironed uniform, a real A-hole. When the line thinned out and he ran out of people to check, he waltzed over to Bob for a chat.

"Howzit chief." Trying to be cool and make friends.

Bob just nodded at him. "Morning."

"Say," said the new guy, "I heard it through the coconut wireless that you and Angie over there split up a while ago, and I was just wondering if you wouldn't mind if I, you know, asked her on a date..." He saw the sudden change in Bob's eyes and stopped midsentence.

"Sure, go ahead," said Bob, his eyes like two dead fish. "And I'll break both your arms..." He picked up two pencils from the desk and broke them very slowly while looking at the new guy. The methodical splintering and cracking of the pencils was actually quite loud and a few people nearby stopped what they were doing and stared. When they were broken completely in half, Bob tossed them in the waste basket. He saw his shift replacement heading towards them, looked at his watch to confirm that his shift was in fact done, dusted the splinters off his lap as he got to his feet and smiled brightly at the new guy, and reiterated, "...in half."

His shift now complete, he high fived his replacement on his way to the side door and almost started skipping and had to restrain himself and looked around, too many people were watching. He was just so damn happy to be off work, and he looked at his watch again to reconfirm, eleven o'clock on the dot, just enough time to grab his clubs from the house and get to the course by noon. He could feel it in his bones, today was gonna be his day. The new guy had riled him up, gotten his blood boiling a bit and now it was time to put a beat down on Harley and the guys. As he walked down the service corridor to the time clock and certain that no one was watching he did a little two step with his happy feet. It was time to play golf, and all was well with the world.

11.

"Mary Beatrice Sun Quan Young!" The woman's voice echoed throughout the little plantation house and filtered out into the immaculate yard that was filled with orchids and flowering ornamental plants, all types and varieties in pots large and small, lined along the edge of the property both on the ground and set on shelves five and seven rows high. Five and seven being a very important number with one set of five shelves filled with plants, then a single pot on the ground, then another row of seven shelves, then a single pot on the ground, and then a row of five shelves filled with pots, and so on and so on.

The old man working in the shade of the Lichee tree tightened his ears to block the sound. He glanced at his watch and saw that it was close to eleven in the morning, too early for someone to be yelling and disturbing his quiet time.

"Mary Beatrice Sun Quan Young!" The voice echoed out into the yard again, and the old man tending to the plants with care looked up and shook his head.

"Ahh," he muttered, hating distractions, and he put down the pruning scissors and looked over at the open field where a young woman was riding a horse, her black hair flowing wildly in the wind. She was practicing a double mugging move between two barrels set fifty feet apart and the horse was sweating and panting to keep up with her demands, and the demands of the whip.

An old woman came to the door of the

plantation house and was ready to call out again when the old man stopped her in her tracks with an upheld hand and an admonition.

"She's out riding; can you not hear the galloping of the hooves on the ground dear one?"

And it was true. The sound of the hooves echoed throughout the countryside as if an army of men on horseback was attacking a fort, so forceful did the young woman ride. The dear one wiped her hands on her apron and smoothed back her hair and smiled, and walked down the steps to join the old man in the green and flowering yard.

"Your plants are looking fine today Papa," she said admiringly.

"They have a mind of their own," said the old man. "Growing out of control." He snipped some wayward leaves that were wrecking havoc with the organized nature of growth that he insisted on. Snip, snip.

"I was hoping Mary Beatrice would be able to go down to the store to get some flour.," said the old woman a little wistfully.

"You mean Bonzai Betty?" Asked the old man and he chuckled when he saw the look on the old woman's face. "Oh, don't be so cross, it's just a nickname."

She frowned at that, and her eyes narrowed as if to say, 'I'll get you for that old man, you just wait and see'. Mrs. Young was a devout Catholic who went to Mass every morning and sipped wine every evening, and loved her Mary Beatrice with all her heart.

Their youngest daughter was named on the very night that she was born, for it was a most difficult delivery for the old woman and nearly cost her with her life. They named her quickly just in case the unspoken were to happen. It was the last child she was able to bear and she forever thought of her as her baby even now that she was full grown and riding a horse like a man.

"Name her after my beloved Grandmother," she had said on that fateful birth night, while barely holding on to this world, and gazing at her baby.

Grandma Mary Beatrice was the blue eyed matriarch of her family who had endured a sailing trip around the horn of South America while a teenager to come to the islands from a Portugal reeling from economic depression in the early part of the last century. Tough and strong willed, she worked her way up from being penniless to owning her own ranch within her lifetime, and that strong willed determination was instilled upon all the children and grandchildren she raised, iron fisted with one hand and bullwhip in the other.

Mary Beatrice was a name as enshrined in the lore of this land as some of the Kings of past. To name her youngest child with that famous name was an honor. How she ever got the nickname Bonzai Betty over the years puzzled the old woman.

Old man Young looked over towards the field and whistled. Old woman Young covered her ears right before the whistle blew, knowing full well in advance what was about to happen. The years of living together fit them as well together as two pieces of a jigsaw puzzle. Mary Beatrice looked over as she was rounding the far barrel and seeing her parents together under the tree and hearing the loud whistle she wheeled her horse and galloped to the fence and parked the horse next to it. She stood on the saddle, and then jumped off the horse and over the fence, landing squarely on her two feet, and smoothed back her long black hair and strode to the tree nearly out of breath.

Old man Young shook his head. How such a beautiful young woman remained unmarried escaped him. All the other children, eight of them in all had been married for a long time and were out on their own, raising families, having children. Any yet Mary Beatrice remained. It was an anomaly that concerned him at times, and he would ponder the question often as he tended to his ornamentals. He didn't mind that she remained at home, and it gave him comfort, and if truth be told some cushion from being alone with his wife in the house. Maybe she just plain scared the hell out of the men with her brazen attitude, he thought, that and her bullwhip. He sighed with an ongoing understanding, for disregarding her beauty; she was about the most hardheaded young woman he had ever seen.

"Hello Momma," said Mary Beatrice as she hugged her mother. She just loved her Mom, always baking and cooking up something fine in the kitchen. "Hello again Poppa," as she patted him on the head. "Did you see that last barrel?"

He scoffed and went back to trimming his plants. "Dip your right shoulder a little lower in the middle of the turn," he said. "That will get you through it quicker."

Her mom winked at her. "Lift up as you exit the turn and that will give the horse more leverage."

Mary Beatrice put up her hand in protest. "Okay, okay, I only wanted to know if you saw the last turn, I didn't ask for a pinpoint critique."

"We only want what's best for you," said her

mother.

"If you wanted what's best for me, you'd let me ride Sweet Streak in the rodeo next week."

"What's wrong with your horse?"

"Amicus? He's okay I guess, better than most, but as you say he needs more leverage out of the turns. He's built more for a long straight runs."

"We'll see," said her Mom. Sweet Streak was a bay colored American Morgan breed, fourteen hands high which was a little shorter than some of the other breeds on the ranch and perfectly suited for barrel racing. She was also Momma Young's horse.

"That horse is just itching to get out there and compete, look how she's pressed against the fence, watching Amicus. You should have seen her run along the fence while we were barrel racing. I thought she was going to jump right over the fence and join us."

"We'll see," said her mother again, and the look on her face meant it.

"Come sit by me for a while," said her Dad. "I want to talk with you since we're all here together in the cool shade of this nice tree. You work so much and are so busy with all your activities. The longest conversation we've had recently has either been 'Hi', or 'Bye'"

He set out the plastic cups and poured three glasses of lemonade while the girls sat at the table.

"Isn't this nice?" he said.

Betty's face scrunched up. "Sour."

"Oh, I ran out of sugar," said her Mom. "Can you run to the store and pick some up along with some flour?"

"Sure Mom."

Old man Young took a sip, and his face slowly grimaced, and he pushed his glass towards his wife. "Put your little pinky in there will you dear, to sweeten it up." His wife giggled and blushed.

"Oh brother," said Betty.

"Your brother David called this morning," said her Dad. "He's coming for Thanksgiving, bringing along the new baby. That means everyone will be here, all eight brothers and sisters, wives and husbands and babies. Twenty three plus us means twenty six at the table. We need one more guest to make it a lucky twenty seven."

"Invite the neighbors."

"That would make twenty eight."

"Maybe you could invite someone."

"I'll think about it."

"Where are they all staying?"

"Your room."

"Funny. Is this the time when you ask me about 'my future', when I'm planning on settling down, and raising a family like the rest of your kids?"

"Not at all, I'm just telling you who's coming to visit for the holiday. Besides, I know you've been going through a rough patch lately."

"I am not going through a 'rough patch' thank you; everything is just fine in my life. I'm working, I'm dancing, and I'm riding Amicus in the rodeo. Everything is fine."

"Ever since what's his name messed up and you had to kick him out on his ear."

"I haven't kicked anyone… yet."

"I never did like that guy anyways."

"Dad, you sat under this tree with him about a hundred times laughing and joking. Telling fart jokes."

"I was pretending to have a good time, for your sake."

"Are we done here?"

"Well I guess since you brought it up, are there any 'potential' new suitors in line?"

"Since I brought it up?"

"Anyone we need to worry about, or keep our eye on?"

"Is that what you call it?"

"For some reason," said her Mom, "your Dad has always looked at you as his baby. The other kids, I guess by the time he had time to come up for air from all the work he was doing, they were already grown up and gone. He looked around and you were all that was left to fuss after."

He nodded. "Remember the first time a boy came to the house to pick you up for a date?"

"Sure, you were sitting under this tree wearing a filthy ripped to shreds shirt, and a mean and dirty scowl on your face while you sharpened your machete."

"I was cleaning the yard. Guys get dirty when they do that."

"You were mumbling incoherently, and waving the machete around like a crazy person."

"There was a bee flying around me. I was trying to swat it."

She pointed at a large gash in the wooden picnic table. "This is where you hacked the table."

He smiled at that, and rubbed his finger on the gash, good times. "That bee was lucky. It landed on the table; I took careful aim, and baaam! The darn machete got stuck, and it took a lot to get it loose. It was kind of like the Sword in the Stone."

"He was afraid to get out of the car, Dad."

"Oh well….."

Momma Young poured some more lemonade in her glass and scrunched her face as she sipped it. "Yow." She put her hand on Betty's and patted it. "Dear, we're just concerned that you're wasting the best time of your life."

"So when I was sixteen you were doing everything you could to chase away any boy who came around here, and now ten years later you're trying to chase me away. Sounds like now you want me to elope with any old Tom, Dick, or Harley who comes along." She realized her mistake and slapped her forehead. "Harry, I meant Tom, Dick or Harry, stupid old saying."

"Maybe you should get out of the house a little more. You know mix it up a little bit instead of sulking around the house."

"I work three jobs Dad. I'm hardly ever home."

Her Mom's face was still sour from the lemonade. "Dear, can you go down to the store and pick up some flour and sugar? I want to sweeten up this juice, and do some baking tonight."

"Sure, maybe the stock clerk will ask me out on a date."

"Is he single?" asked her Dad.

Her face drained of expression, and she held out her hand, palm up.

They looked at her blankly for a moment. "Oh, right," said her Dad and reached in his pocket for his wallet. He patted his back pockets, then his front ones, and then with a puzzled look on his face looked around underneath the chair. "My wallet, my wallet…"

Betty face still had not regained a single iota of

expression as she watched the charade. What the hell was it with guys and their wallets? Finally she just shook her head, and pulled her empty hand back. "Never mind, I've got it." She slowly got up out of the chair and walked back to the corral, and even though the gate was right there she climbed to the top of the fence, and hopped on Amicus.

"Thanks dear," her mother shouted at her, but she didn't look back, just gave the horse a little nudge with her heels to get him trotting, and then suddenly gave him a quick whip on the haunches and yelled "Hyaaahh!" and Amicus took off like a bolt of lightning towards the opposite fence by the road, jumped clear over it and galloped off towards town in a ball of swirling dust.

"That girl worries me," said her Dad.

"Me too," said her Mom. "Amicus is plenty of horse for her to ride in the rodeo. Did you see how he cleared that fence?"

"By at least three feet," he said. "Makes you wonder sometimes, about her judgment and all."

"Well," her mother said, recalling an old Portagee cowboy saying. "Maybe she'll grow into her boots."

"Let's hope so," said her Dad as he went back to snipping his Bonzai tree. "We're not getting any younger. I'd hate to see her grow into an old maid."

Betty rode as fast as Amicus would take her towards the little town. The dirt trail next to the road was well worn from her many rides into town with nary a stone or pebble in the way.

Every time she thought about her recent conversation with her father she gave out a yell and a quick switch to Amicus' backside, and the horse galloped faster.

The speed limit on that stretch of road was twenty five miles an hour and Amicus was going about thirty five. They passed a police car parked on the other side of the road; the officer was giving a traffic ticket to a depressed driver who pointed at the horse as it flew by.

"What about that guy?" moaned the driver, obviously from out of town.

The officer looked up when he heard the stampeding horse trample by, and laughed at the comment. "You're lucky she didn't hear you say that pal. Here's your ticket." He handed the slip of paper to the hapless driver as a cloud of dust enveloped them, and he shook his head as he walked back to the patrol car, he'd seen Betty bullwhip guys for less than that what that guy had just said. He watched as the whirling ball of dust disappeared down the road and whistled. "Damn that's a hell of a woman right there."

As Betty got closer to the town, she eased back on the reigns, and Amicus slowed to a trot. He was breathing hard and flecks of foam jetted from the side of his mouth. "Easy now boy, that's good, good Amicus." She soothed him with her voice and brought him up to the fence next to the post office and hopped off. There was a spigot nearby for the flowers and she turned it on and filled a large bowl that she kept there. Amicus leaned his head down and drank heartily while Betty stroked his mane until she was sure he was cooling down. It was good to ride a horse hard once in a while; it kept them and the rider in top shape. She took a deep breath and relaxed having ridden the rile out of herself.

In a town this small it wasn't uncommon for

everyone in the nearby community to pass through at least once in the day, going to the post office, or the store, or the school, or the library, or to get gas, or catch the bus, or pick up a plate lunch from the snack shop, it was the hub of the south side of the island and at this of the day, right before lunch was one of the busiest times of the day. By the time Betty reached the little store she had either waved at or been whistled at more than two dozen times, and she'd only walked a hundred feet. There were two stores in the town, the big nationwide conglomerate with the big shiny windows, all air conditioned and giant on one side of town, and the little mom and pop store that had been on the same corner for over a hundred years, quaint and a little dusty around the corners, but usually had some good items on sale to lure the customers in.

She meandered through the front door and sized up the fruit and vegetables, and then the dairy section. The prices were astronomical, and she thanked her lucky stars that they had a big vegetable garden in the yard and a milk cow in the field. Old man Young, though stingy as could be with his cash, even with his own daughter, was pretty smart to set up the little farm as he had. The only food items he didn't grow were grain for flour, and hops and grapes for beer and wine. Everything else they could just go out in the yard and gather up.

As luck would have it there were five types of flour, and there was one on sale, unbleached. She cradled the little sack of flour like a baby, picked up a box of sugar and headed for the checkout line, and as luck would have it again, as she headed out the front door she ran into Marlena and Archie walking hand in hand. She tried to hide behind a pillar, but Marlena spotted her and poked her in the arm.

"Hey you, trying to hide eh?"

"You caught me." She smiled at her friend and then nodded. " Hi Archie."

Archie nearly fell backwards on the ground, holding onto his chest near his heart, and Marlena pulled him upright, "C'mon, cut it out Mr. Drama King."

Betty had actually greeted him, and in a nice way. "Well hello there," he said. "Did you have fun the other night?"

"The food was good."

"Gotta love that Cave barbecue. I know it must have been kind of a surprise for you to see me there with Marlena."

"Shocked is more like it. She's been keeping you a secret."

"Yeah, well I think everyone was a little bit shocked. The secret is out I guess. How in the world anyone could keep a secret in this little town is beyond me, and we really didn't try to make it a secret anyways. Meeting at the Cave was fun, and it was nice to see you and Harley talking again, at least you were talking. I always figured you two might be able to work things out."

Her fist and her jaw clenched simultaneously and she replied slowly. "Oh we worked things out quite a while ago actually." Her mind filled with a vision of Harley asking girl after girl for her phone number while laughing and laughing, a nightmare come to life, and she tried to block out the vision but it was there in the front of her mind. She instinctively reached for her bullwhip and then realized in a daze that she wasn't on her horse.

Amicus was parked across the street with his head in the water bucket. She came out of her dark haze and took a deep breath, and let it out slowly. "All worked out, thanks for asking though." That's it, all better now; she breathed and breathed, all better, all better....

"You know," continued Archie, "I was thinking about having a little dinner party at the new restaurant in town, inviting the usual suspects, my golfing buddies, and of course Marlena and her friends. It'd be fun."

Betty snapped her fingers. "Aw shucks, I have plans."

"Yeah?"

"I was going to work on some things. You know the old saying, make hay while the sun shines."

"But it'll be night," joked Archie.

"Well the sun's always shining somewhere."

Archie laughed. "My motto is, when the sun's shining play golf."

"Please come with us," pleaded Marlena and pulled at her hand.

"I'll make sure the guys are on their best behavior," said Archie. "Especially Harley."

"Hey look," said Marlena. "Speaking of the devil, there's Harley now." The old truck ambled up Main Street past the big store and the post office and turned on the road that headed up the hill towards the golf course. He drove right past them and kept his eyes straight on the road, even with Marlena jumping up and down, waving her arms, and yelling his name. Harley kept right on driving without turning his head or acknowledging them.

"Well he must be the most careful driver in the world," marveled Marlena, and then narrowed her eyes. "Or else he's ignoring us."

"He's got his game face on," said Archie. "I'm surprised he didn't flip us the bird."

Marlena's face reddened. "I know what the flip of the bird means, but what's a game face?"

"You know like this," said Archie, and he let all the muscles in his face go slack, let all expression drain out, and then made his face look mean, his lower lip trembled and his eye twitched. Marlena got up close and studied him carefully, and then burst out laughing which made Archie break down and laugh along with her.

Betty felt like she was standing with a couple of lunatics on the corner, people walking by were staring at them. It was embarrassing.

In his rear view mirror as he was driving up the hill Harley could see them at the corner of the store, laughing and laughing. They were probably laughing at him. His hands tightened on the wheel. This is what he could expect from now on unless he changed the way things were going. "Go ahead laughing boy," he said as they faded from sight. "Yuk it up." Then he punched the accelerator to the floor and the truck bolted up the road towards the course.

"But what does it mean, to have a game face?" asked Marlena.

Archie frowned. "I really do have a lot to teach you don't I? Okay, it means to not let the other guy know what you're thinking, never give him an edge, you know, a psychological edge when you're in a sporting match."

"You're in a sporting match?"

"No not now, but we will be about half an hour. It's almost noon, it's time for our golf match."

12.

Her Dad was a cop. Her brother was a cop. Even her Mom was a cop until she had two kids and decided it was best to stay home and cook and clean.

So when they told Angie she couldn't be a cop, it came as a surprise.

"You're too short," said the recruiter sitting behind the desk. "Minimum height is five foot two."

"That's me," she said. "Five-two."

"Says five-one on the physical."

"What the hell?" She reached over the desk and turned the sheet to read it. Height: five one. "It's a mistake," she said. "I'm five-two in my bare feet. You got a tape measure in that drawer? Measure me against that wall and I'll prove it."

"No can do Angie, we gotta go with the Doc's report. Go home and eat your vitamins and drink your milk and come back next year." He grinned at her.

"Next year? I'll see you next week chump."

During the physical she'd been more worried about her weight and forgot to look at the height they'd written down. If she stood ramrod straight and stretched the bones from her ankles to her head she was just about five-two.

She went on-line and found some barefoot lifts for just this situation, obviously she wasn't the only one who'd been in this predicament. Skin colored, you glued them on the bottom of your heels and used putty to blend them into your natural skin. There was always a way around a problem if you used your wits. No one even looks at your feet when standing on the scale for a height measurement.

"What's that?" said the nurse with concern on her face as Angie stood on the scale for her second run at the physical.

"What's what?" Angie was impatient to get this over with and take the paper with the five-two on it and shove it in the recruiter's face.

"That thing on your heel, my God it looks painful."

Angie looked down and caught her breath. As she was standing and straining to make the height, the heel lift created an air bubble that pushed out from the edge of the putty and looked like a giant blister.

"I'll go get the doctor," said the nurse as she quickly left the room, "maybe he can pop it."

Angie turned to stop her, "Oh it's nothing..." But it was too late. She bent down to smooth out the bubble and when she stood back up was afraid to move for fear the bubble would come back. When the nurse came back in the room with Dr. Brock and pointed to the offensive heel, Angie smiled sheepishly. "It's a miracle, it just disappeared."

The good old doctor who delivered her as a baby was concerned and nestled his reading glasses on his nose and knelt down. "Well let's have a look shall we, just to be on the safe side." He gently touched the heel and looked at his finger with the flesh colored putty and tapped gently on the fake heel.

"Tsk tsk," he said as he shook his head, sorely disappointed. "Really now Angie, fudging on the physical? I'll tell you what, how about I print up some healthy tips on gaining an inch in height the natural way, and we'll just keep this between us."

Two years later she was still an inch too short, and although the good doctor kept his word, the nurse turned out to be a big fat blabbermouth and everyone on the island knew she tried to cheat on the exam. So now she had to have a 'special screening' if she ever tried for another physical.

"We'll get you in over at the airport," said her Dad. "I know some of the guys. It's nice steady work, and will look good on your resume when you finally do grow into your feet." Talking to her like she was a dog or something.

Two years wearing this stupid orange vest. And people wondered why airport cops had a bad attitude.

Traffic was running smooth for a Wednesday morning. She was in the middle of the entrance area, across from the Agriculture Inspection station, in the crosswalk, white gloved hands moving the cars forward, whistle on her lips at the ready. The traffic light at the intersection had been broken for the past month and she was the one stuck with the duty, waving cars through or making them stop when pedestrians needed to get across, like a human crosswalk light, it was humiliating. Normally she would be on foot patrol in the parking lot, or along the embarkment curbs telling people what to do, or not to do, to move along, writing tickets, giving warnings, the fun stuff. Here in the middle of the intersection she was like a cigar store Indian with just about as much power, while in the corner of her eyes she could see a smug Bob sitting in his chair, like a king on his throne, pulling people out of line on a whim, making them walk the plank if he wanted. She looked at her watch and saw that it was nearly eleven, and that meant he'd be heading off to play golf with the other losers. Good, she thought, I won't have to look at him sitting there all high and mighty. Everything used to be just fine between them, until the day he made the mistake of telling a short joke.

Maybe it wouldn't have been so bad if she hadn't had to endure her two brother's endlessly ribbing her on missing out on the entry requirements every single chance they got. Sure they all grew up in a small house and had to fight over everything just to survive, food, water, the bathroom. Space was limited and it was every man or woman for themselves when it came to some things. Battles won and lost somehow carried over and never really ended, they just turned into new opportunities to battle.

"Don't worry," said one brother, "I heard it through the grapevine that you're on the short list to be hired next year."

"Wow," said the other brother, "they really gave you the short end of the stick on that one didn't they?"

"Good thing you don't have a short temper, or they'd be in big trouble." Etc.

Even her Dad tried to get into the act, thinking he was being funny and lightening up the situation.

"Don't worry pumpkin," he said. "I know without a doubt that you'll succeed at whatever you do. Just remember one thing, there's no shortcut to the top."

You had to have pretty thick skin to grow up in a house with a bunch of cops running the show. Not only did you have to have thick skin, but you had to be able to dish out the punishment equally in order to survive. So when her boyfriend Bob made the mistake of a mis-timed wisecrack it was the end of the road for him.

They were out on a dinner date right after she got turned down for the job for the fifth and potentially last time. She was still a half inch too short.

"You gotta be kidding me!" she yelled at the doctor. "What are you using to measure me with, an atomic laser device?"

Bob was sympathetic and offered to take her to dinner to cheer her up.

"Just think," he said. "Now we can see each other all the time." Which really meant that he could keep an eye on her day and night. He had a bit of a jealous streak in him.

After a nice dinner the bill came and Bob reached for his wallet as expected, after all he was the one who asked her on the date in the first place. He fumbled around for a while and mumbled something under his breath.

"Do you have enough money, I can help," she offered, reaching for her purse.

"Well if you don't mind, I'll pay you back tomorrow, I'm just a little bit short at the moment."

The instant he said it time seemed to stand still and much as he tried, he couldn't retrieve the words as they were leaving his mouth in slow motion, and realized it was horrible mistake. "Whoops." Maybe she didn't even notice what he said, he thought. And then he laughed a little, nervously. It was the laugh that was the final nail in his coffin, and she calmly got up and walked out without another word and never spoke to him again.

Traffic was moving slowly through the airport and she stopped thinking about the past. What was done was done. It's the present that matters most, she thought. Just live for today.

A large SUV caught her attention. It pulled up to the curb and a middle aged woman stepped out of the passenger side and went to one of the airline ticketing lines.

Angie walked over to it and tapped on the driver's side window and the man rolled it down.

"Sir, you'll have to move this vehicle, you can't stay parked here."

"I'm waiting for my wife, she's right over there."

"She's waiting in a long line sir, that will take quite awhile."

"That's okay, I'm not in a hurry. Hey, just hang loose, right?" He gave her the shaka sign and smiled, she could see his gold fillings in the back of his mouth.

"I'm sorry sir but this is a no parking zone and you're blocking half the cross walk, you'll have to move."

He pulled out his wallet and showed her his I.D. Government issue. District of Columbia. House of Representatives.

"So you're in Congress?"

"On vacation. Wonderful island you have here. I think we'll come back again someday for a longer visit. One week just isn't long enough to see everything you know."

An old lady with a cane limped around his front bumper to gain access to the crosswalk and gave the driver a dirty look. Angie leaned closer to the congressman.

"Sir, could you just move this vehicle to the parking lot while you wait for your wife?"

"Why would I want to move the car when I am parked in such an advantageous place? My wife is right there in line to pick up our tickets to get on the flight this afternoon. Normally I'd just have my assistant print out our boarding passes, but we're travelling alone this time."

Angie could tell he was stalling for time, she'd seen this tactic before. She pointed down the road. "Sir you can pull into the parking lot right over there to wait, there's no charge if it's less than fifteen minutes. I'm sure it won't take that long for your wife to pick up the tickets."

"How old are you?" he asked.

"How old am I?"

He looked her up and down and continued. "I was just wondering how old you were and all, considering that it's a school day. Isn't it a Wednesday morning? Aren't you supposed to be in class?"

Angie's face began to turn red as the man continued. "Let me give you a little lesson. I am a United States Congressman, I've shown you my identification, I have diplomatic immunity at any port or transportation hub within our nation's borders to ingress and egress at will without being impeded by any law enforcement personnel for any reason whatsoever. Now why don't you just run along now and find some other meter maids to play with." He smiled and the window silently rolled up.

A small crowd gathered around the car, watching the action. She tapped on the window with her finger. Nothing. She made a fist and pounded on it with four knuckles. A police officer on the other side of the road saw the commotion and started walking their way.

He rolled down the window. His smile was gone. "Now listen here short stuff, I've had just about enough of this nonsense."

Short stuff.

She had to move fast while the window was still down and reached with both hands behind her waist for the mace and the taser that were hooked to her belt, not sure which she was going to use first, and then as she got a solid grip on both and had the triggers secure and ready to fire she had a brilliant idea: 'Why not both at once?'

13.

Rivalries develop when competitors play each other over and over and over again, and that was the situation with our combatants. Even though it was Wednesday to most of the working world, the middle of the week, hump day, get over it, through it however which way you needed to get to the other side of it day, and it was all downhill to the weekend and fun time day, whatever nickname you wanted to give Wednesday. For Harley and Archie and Josh and Bob, Wednesday was just another day. When it was high noon on the island it was time to rev your engines, tee 'em up, and battle it out. They were all evenly matched enough in ability, and over the years had tried just about every gimmick to get an advantage over the other guys.

One day before heading to the course, Harley made a sandwich with fresh onions, fresh jalapeños, and as an afterthought added one fresh chopped garlic and ate it before the match. He never thought much about it, as far as he was concerned he was just making a tasty treat in the middle of the day.

After he conveyed his usual greetings to his fellow competitors on the tee and turned down their request for strokes, they all turned green and gave him a wide berth throughout the day, and he won handily. The next day, thinking he was pretty smart, he tried the same trick, only this time with two cloves of garlic in the sandwich, however 'ol Archie in a brilliant counter move secretly ate twenty cloves of raw garlic in the parking lot, and after one giant burp on the first tee, set Josh and Bob to hurling in the bushes. All the tourists standing nearby who witnessed the scene cancelled their tee times and went home, and the greens keepers had to hose down the tee box, and the course lost money. After some prodding from the course marshal and the threat of a year long ban, they all agreed to a standing rule against the excessive use of garlic.

The par four eighth hole plays straight uphill against the wind and is the hardest hole on the course.

The ball rocketed off Archie's driver and down the left side of the fairway.

"Hit a tree," said Harley.

"HIT THE TREE," said Josh as the ball headed towards a towering pine.

Archie cringed and leaned to the right, hopping on one leg, waving his hand and coaxing the ball in flight.

Keeraaack, it hit dead center on the Norfolk pine and bounced backwards towards the tee, a monster fifty yard drive.

"SON OF A MOTHER!" shouted Archie. "That's dirty pool talking to my ball." He glared at Bob and Josh who were bent over laughing.

"Tell it not to listen," said Harley as he teed up his ball and got ready to hit it. He stood well behind the ball and lined up his shot, and took a practice swing and envisioned the flight path straight up the fairway. Slowly and with great purpose and rhythm he stepped up to the ball, got into his stance and quietly, almost in a hypnotic trance he settled his feet. All was golden silence around him. He looked once more down the fairway, secure in his aim and brought the club back for a mighty swing, and out of the corner of his eye he saw Archie doing a monkey dance behind him, hat skewed sideways, tongue sticking out, lunging from side to side, arms dangling widely.

"What the hell?" shouted Harley as he tried to stop his swing without tearing his arm out of the socket, and he spun around nearly falling to the ground. "Now that is dirty pool!" he yelled. "At least I wait until the ball's in the air."

"He does that every time you hit the ball," said Bob to laughter. Archie and Josh were rolling on the grass again, out of breath.

"You know there's a big difference between distracting a ball in flight, and the guy actually hitting the ball?"

"You weren't supposed to see the monkey dance," said Archie as he gasped for air.

Harley stepped back to the ball and blocking any thought of a monkey dance on stage behind him, fired a drive up the middle. It hung in the air and fell just past Josh and Bob's shots.

They travelled the short distance to Archie's wayward tee shot and waited for him to choose a club.

"Par four my rear end," said Archie as he got ready to hit his second shot. He was still three hundred yards from the green and still up uphill against the wind to get there, which made it more like four hundred yards.

"Play it like a par five," said Harley. "And quit bitching. Hit it halfway to the green, pitch it up and two putt for bogey," he said. "And then watch me as I get on in two and par," he said as an aside just loud enough for Archie to hear it.

"Check out where his ball is sitting," said Bob. Just to the right of Archie's ball was the ladies tee, the red markers. "You know the rule, if you don't hit it past the ladies tee, you have to wear your shorts around your ankles for the remainder of the hole."

Sure enough, as they all took a close second look, the ball looked to be a fraction behind the red tees. They all huddled on the side as though they were land surveyors.

"Not past the red tees," proclaimed Harley.

"No, you guys are definitely wrong on this one," said Archie. "It's exactly even with the tees, see if you look close you can see that all three are perfectly lined up.

"So you're saying that your ball is lined up even with the red markers?" asked Harley.

"What'd I just say?" said Archie who was beginning to get perturbed. "Is there an echo out here? Yes, my ball is even with the red markers and therefore has in effect passed the red markers. It's kind of like in tennis, if the ball touches the line, it's in."

"It's out," said Bob. "If it touches the line it's out."

"In," said Archie.

"Out," repeated Bob.

"We're saying that your ball has to travel past the line to be past the red markers," said Harley, "And you're saying that it only has to *touch* the line to be in the field of play because the line *is* in the field of play and is part of the field, and we're saying that the line is out of the field of play and not part of it."

"Exactly, now if you'll excuse me I have a shot

to play."

Harley put out his hand and stopped Archie from walking towards his ball, he had a cell phone in his hand. It was ringing and he put it on speakerphone.

"Island tennis club, this is Alberto can I help you?"

"Alberto I have a quick rules question for you," said Harley loudly. "If the tennis ball touches the line is it in, or out."

"Out," said Alberto. "That's an easy one, if a fraction of the ball touches a fraction of the line, it's out. You see in pro matches they have a sensor that…"

Harley hung up the phone and shook his head. "Well, that settles that."

Due to the lengthy discussion of the red tee ruling, the group behind them had already caught up and the two men in the group were standing with their hands on their hips impatiently ready to play. Archie looked back at them and sighed. In the same group were a couple of women, still seated in their golf carts, waiting for their husbands to hit their shots so they could move up to the red tee that was currently the site of an ugly legal proceeding.

Archie took a deep breath and pulled out a club.

"Driver off the deck," he announced, then unbuttoned his shorts and dropped them to the ground. His legs were now hindered by the shorts, and he couldn't get a solid stance but he set his game face and settled in for his penalty shot. His undershorts, which were a present from Marlena sported a large pink heart which stared them in the face, and being the gentlemen they were, stifled their snickering while the shot was attempted.

They all watched in silence as Archie took a smooth swing at the ball, the trampoline sized face of the club hitting it flush with distinctive 'ping' sound.

"That's right!" shouted Archie as the ball flew straight and true, low and under the wind just a few feet off the ground and rolled up onto the green. He pumped his fist and pointed at Harley, then pulled up his pants.

"We're all getting a little tired of your little driver off the deck action," said Harley as they continued up the fairway.

As it turned out, it was Harley who got the par, while Archie and others scored bogeys, cutting into Archie's lead. With eight holes in the books and one to go, Archie was up by one and could win the match, but Harley was on a roll and could tie him by winning the last hole.

And then something happened that could only be described as miraculous, and would be henceforth and from then on be referred to by the group as the 'Man Diaper Incident'.

Harley had a habit of visiting the lua, otherwise known as the bathroom, that was situated in between the eighth and ninth holes and the guys usually had to wait for a length of time that they referred to simply as 'too long'. A year or two back Bob had a few too many beverages, got fed up and started ramming the outhouse with the cart and got banned from the course for a month. Harley took partial blame and promised to make his 'trips' a little more economical and time savvy. This time Harley went in the door and came right back out looking pale as a sheet. They all laughed at the look on his face.

"It's not funny," said Harley

"You look like you just saw a ghost," said Archie.

Josh was afraid of ghosts and quickly stopped laughing. "Wait, you really didn't see one, did you?"

"Depends," said Harley.

"Depends on what?" Josh was becoming concerned and sat straight up in the cart.

Harley mumbled 'Depends' again, and then shut his eyes and slapped himself repeatedly on the forehead, trying to get the image out of his mind. It was no use. He started walking for the next tee, foregoing his bathroom break.

Josh looked at the door of the lua and started after him, pulling at his shoulder. "Hey c'mon Harley, what the heck? What did you see in there?"

"Depends," said Harley again, and then stopped so he could give his full attention to Josh who was bugging the heck out of him. "Depends, you know - man diapers, draped over the toilet paper dispenser. The guy didn't even have the courtesy to throw them in the trash."

They all laughed.

Harley kept walking and explained in a slow serious voice.

"When I was a kid my old Grandpa would come for visits every summer and stay for about a month or so. It was great, he had so many stories to tell, and he took us to get ice cream every day. He usually got pretty comfortable around the house and sometimes forgot to put on his shirt or what not, left his false teeth on the kitchen table, you know things like that. One day he came walking out of his room with no pants. He was wearing no pants. No kid should have to see that. I almost dropped my cereal on the floor, I'll never forget that day; I was just ten. He forgot to put on his dang pants guys. And he was wearing a giant diaper. He just laughed and explained the whole inconsonant factor in a man's life. 'It's a fate that befalls a man, he said. If a man lives to be old.'"

Harley kept walking, quiet as he could, closing his eyes now and then and slapping his head. "It's a fate that I fear awaits me," he finally said as they got to the next tee.

Now Harley should have known better than to disclose any critical, personal details about his life that were unbeknownst to the others while they were at the end of a grueling match, especially a detail that was so close to home for him. It was an unwritten rule of golf that needling your opponent prior to them setting up for their next shot was not only acceptable behavior, it was expected.

"Well," said Archie, as Harley strode towards the tee. "The only fate that I fear awaits you is the vision of those Man Diapers at the very moment you're hitting your drive."

Harley closed his eyes and tried to shut down the function of his ears, fill his mind with static, noise, close off the world around him, and live in a bubble until he hit his ball.

Josh winked at Bob and asked loudly. "How long is this hole playing today?"

"Depends," said Bob.

"Depends on what?"

"Well it depends on where the flagstick is on the green, it depends on the wind coming from the East, it depends on so many factors that I cannot rightly say exactly how long this hole is playing today. It just depends."

Harley teed up his ball and closed his eyes, trying to envision something, anything loud and mind numbing; a dragster blowing off the line, wheels smoking fire and rubber, the engine ready to explode from the torque; a basketball rim shattering slam dunk; a cracking home run hit with the crowd roaring in the background. He ran an old Alice Cooper song through his mind conjuring up the brain numbing electric chord vibrations of 'Schools out for Summer', humming the words and gritting his teeth, and finally satisfied in his isolated and aggressive attitude with a swirl of background noise in his brain, he sighted his line down the fairway, set his feet rock solid, focused his eyes on the ball, took the club back straight and sloooow on his backswing, locked his wrists at the top, pushed off his back foot, and swung mightily in a perfect downward arc, and at the exact moment the club hit the ball a flash of light filled with a giant diaper was in the front of his mind and he shanked his drive into the woods.

Bushes and flowers surrounding the tee box wilted under the crescendo of expletives that followed. Birds flying nearby in the sky diverted quickly from the area, while the navigator in an airliner high above in the stratosphere noticed the instrument gauges oscillate and tapped on them, and a vacationing fishing captain from Alaska who was on the adjacent fairway nodded his approval of the colorful swearing that would fit in well with any ship at sea, and could make even the most seasoned sailor feel right at home.

Harley picked up his tee and ignored the

combatants rolling with glee on the grass and stood on the side in a dark mood. He was sitting behind the proverbial eight ball, one down with one to go and now he was in the dreaded Black Forest on the last hole. If he couldn't beat Archie today of all days he might never get another chance. With Paris looming on the very next day, and a newlywed and neutered Archie unable to ever play again, this was it, the last hurrah, the big shebang. It was time to pull out his secret weapon. He walked over to his golf bag; opened one of the little side pockets, and pulled out a small cloth doll about the size of his palm.

Archie noticed Harley holding something and squinted his eyes from up on the tee box. "Is that a voodoo doll?"

Harley was silent.

"Hey Archie," said Josh, "it kind of looks like you."

Bob laughed. "Hey it really does; blond hair and all." And then he stopped laughing and narrowed his eyes. "That's kind of creepy Harley, you better not have any other ones in there, for instance one that looks like me."

Harley was silent and a sinister crooked smile appeared on his face.

"That's dirty pool," said Archie.

Harley was whispering into the dolls ear. "Hit it out of bounds; hit it out of bounds..." over, and over, and over again.

"That's not how it works," said Josh. "You're supposed to stick little needles in it."

"Yeah and do a little dance while you twist the needles," said Bob.

"Don't give him any ideas," said Archie.

Harley's sinister smile widened as he pulled out a pair of pliers and grabbed onto the dolls hand.

"Don't do it!" shouted Archie.

Harley squeezed the hand with the pliers and kept whispering in the dolls ear. "Out of bounds, out of bounds…"

"You're insane," said Archie, and he teed up his ball and got ready to hit his drive. The tee box got eerily silent as it was definitely poor sportsmanship to be making any noise be it talking, or joking, or whispering to your voodoo doll while someone was actually hitting the ball. Anything up to that point in time was fair gamesmanship, any ribbing you could muster could and should be brought to the table while the other guy was stepping into the tee box, but when a guy actually got ready to hit the ball, it was quiet on the tee, or else. Archie pricked his ears up ready to call an infraction, and finally satisfied that no voodoo whispering was occurring behind him he took his backswing high and tight and swung down at the ball. It cracked off the face of the driver low and straight and very long, and then began veering a little to the right, going to the right, to the right, to the right. "Don't go to the right," shouted Archie.

Now, once a guy hits his ball all shenanigans are once more fair game, and Archie could hear the whispering getting louder and louder, "go out of bounds, out of bounds, out, out, out…"

His ball caught a gust of wind and curved and kept curving, and was headed for the wall that lined the cliff on the right. Archie slumped his shoulders and resigned himself to the inevitable, and then with the luck of the Irish at the very moment it was crossing out of bounds: it HIT the white stake on top of the wall and bounced back into the center of the fairway.

Archie jumped in the air with a fist pump, ran over to Harley and shouted heartily at the little doll, flecks of spittle flying from the corners of his mouth. "In your face! IN YOUR FACE! YEAH, YEAH, YEAH!" Archie's face was beet red from yelling and pumping his fist at the doll.

Harley shook his head and frowned as he put the voodoo doll back into the side pouch. "Wow, that's pretty immature don't you think Archie, yelling at a little doll?"

The ninth hole was the either the hardest hole on the golf course, or the easiest, depending on where your tee shot landed. For the old Captain who long ago perished while trying to cut the corner with his drive from the tee, it was obviously and painfully the hardest hole on the course. For Harley, now deep in the woods on the left side of the fairway, down by one with one to go, and without a clear shot towards the green, his fate was nearly sealed. He had two choices, one was to take his medicine right here and now and hit a little punch shot between two Norfolk pines to just get it back to the fairway where he could try for the miracle long iron over the cliff to the green in three, or he could try for a big sweeping fade through and over a stand of Koa trees, fading it over the fairway, cutting the near the side of the cliff, and run it close to the edge of the green in two. Either way it would take every bit of skill and luck he could muster to pull it off and tie the score on this, the last hole at the end of the world as they knew it. He could see Josh and Bob waiting in the center of the fairway for him to make his decision and Archie standing with them, smug as usual with victory nearly in hand, or was it a big smile? It was hard to tell from here.

There was one other choice, and that one was the most impossible of all, but as he looked at his ball sitting up on some pine needles, and then where he needed to hit it, the possibility dawned on him.

Instead of hitting a punch shot to get to the fairway and *then* hitting over the cliff to the green, why not hit a big shot, the biggest of his life, through the trees and over the cliff to the green and make it there in two? With a driver off the deck from the Black Forest no less. No one had ever even thought about attempting this shot before, it was too far, it was too impossible, it was too crazy. Harley steeled his eyes and pulled the driver.

"He's pulling the driver," said Bob from the fairway.

"Driver off the deck!" yelled Josh.

'It's the driver', muttered Archie. Oh well, let the chips fall where they may. If Harley made it over the cliff to the green it would be the gnarliest shot anyone had ever seen. If he missed, it would just be a miss, so either way it was a good play. Where Archie sat in the middle of the fairway and with the bounce he'd gotten, he had an easy shot to the green in two, and an eagle three was in the cards. It was now or nothing.

Harley took a wide stance in the pine needles and sighted his line through the pine trees towards the green in the distance. It was so far away it was hard to see clearly but he could almost make out the flag waving in the breeze.

"Here goes nothing," he whispered and pulled

the club back ever so softly, hesitated at the top for a split second and then swung smooth and powerfully at the ball and absolutely cranked it. The golf ball split the trees in half and rose through the air like a jet taking off, straight and smooth, gaining altitude and distance and heading over the cliff and towards the green on the other side of the canyon.

His companions watched as it sailed high over their heads.

"Holy cow," whispered a stunned Archie as he watched the magnificent flight of the ball clear the canyon and hover for a moment over the green on its way down.

Harley ran out of the trees and onto the fairway to get a better look, his face not believing what he was seeing.

A gust of wind from the cliff pushed the ball forward and it hit the pin straight on. They could all hear the clank from where they were standing.

"What a shot!" yelled Bob and Josh at the same time, but Harley winced as the ball hit the flag dead on and bounced backwards towards the cliff, bounced again on a sprinkler head and over the wall and into the canyon. It was over. His long streak of wins gone forever. And just when you'd expect a nearly triumphant Archie to gloat at his misfortune, he turned to Harley and tipped his hat.

"It was a great shot. Best I've ever seen. Just a tough break is all."

Bob and Josh being farther back on the fairway hit layup shots just short of the green, but safe, while Archie hit a long iron into the middle of the green, and was sitting there in two, with a bonafide chance at an eagle three, and even if he three putted, he'd be in with a par five score and the win.

Harley dropped his ball close to the lava rock wall where his second shot passed over the cliff and the canyon. If he could sink this shot from two hundred yards out, and Archie three putted for a five, Harley would win the hole and tie the match. "Two in, three out, hitting four," he announced, settling into his stance, and gave it a good swat with a three iron. The ball sailed high over the canyon heading straight for the pin again, another gust of wind hit it, but this time blowing against it, and holding it up and dumping it unceremoniously into the canyon again.

Harley got out another ball, dropped it quickly in the same spot. "Four in, five out, hitting six." And this time the ball sailed through the air with the greatest of ease and landed on the green and stayed there. Harley held his head high as he strolled to the green. He was on in six, and could hole out his putt for a seven. Archie would have to six putt to card an eight, it was still possible, remotely possible, but still a long shot, but then he drilled his eagle putt for a three to end Harley's dreaming.

Archie did a little jig in the parking lot while holding the two quarters high for everyone to see and admire. Harley's reign of terror was finally over and Archie was now the King of the course.

"Never thought I'd see the day again!" shouted Archie in the obligatory celebration that ensued while relishing the quarters held tight in his hands.

Strangers walking by clapped their hands and offered congratulations for obviously this was a great victory.

Harley was magnanimous in defeat. He dipped his hand deep into the ice and pulled out the coldest beer he could find and opened it for Archie. "Nice round buddy. Now when can I get my revenge?"

14.

"Welcome to the Swamp, would you like to hear the specials?" The young man stood next to their table wearing overalls with no undershirt, a straw hat, a corncob pipe sticking out of a front pocket and a sprig of grass in his hair.

Harley looked up from the drink menu and almost fell out of his chair. He caught himself just in time. "Really, a hillbilly server? Well how 'bout you jes fetch us a couple of pitchers of beer there Jethro to start us off."

Archie gave him an elbow and a scowl. "C'mon Harley, this should be good, we want to hear the specials."

"Yeah, c'mon Harley," said Josh, "the young man's only doing his job."

The girls just stared at Harley with disgust which was fine with him, he'd lost the match today and was no mood to be pleasant.

"Alright, alright I'm sorry," he said to the server. "How's yer paw?"

The young man smiled, "He's okay Uncle Harley, working out at the base full time."

"That's good, that's good, they treating you okay round these here parts?"

"Yeah, we're working out the kinks and all. We just opened up a couple of days ago you know."

"That's why we're here. Heard some talk about a mighty fine spread."

"We've got some bluegrass music later, there's a guy with a banjo and another with violin, a keg bass, a singer that does some yodeling, real authentic sounding. They got the Hillbilly bar over there, I mean over yonder, and they got mash whiskey, a corn still, you know the works."

"How's the food?"

"It's uh, you know, uh…"

They all laughed at his indecision.

"Uh oh," said Harley. "It's not *really* road kill is it?"

"No, it's super good, it's just different, they're going for a theme here you know."

Harley sat back and spread his hands. "Alright there Clem, hit us up, what do you got on the special tonight?"

He looked down at his notes. "Alright folks, we got crawdads, king frog legs, alligator steak, mincemeat pie, catfish with lemon butter, taters and grits fresh off the skillet, apple pie and fritters. Plus there's a full menu with any kind of steak and fish combo, just like at a regular restaurant."

"You lost me at the frog legs," said Bob. "Are you kidding me?"

"I know, that's what everyone says."

Harley nodded at Marlena. "You're an international sort of gal, do you eat frog legs?"

"Now and then, but I draw the line at snails."

"Alright," said Archie. "Why don't you bring out a couple of pitchers of beer and we'll look over the menu."

"I'll have a glass of chardonnay," said Melissa.

"Me too," chimed Angie.

"Smart move," said Josh and patted his belly. "Beer's fattening."

Angie's face reddened. "What's really fat is the space between your ears." She grabbed her glass of water and got ready to heave it across the table.

"Now now children," said Marlena as she held up her hand and smiled at the waiter, "I'll take a glass of merlot."

"Better hurry with the drinks," said Archie. "And bring some pupus while you're at it" He looked quickly at the menu. "We'll take a couple of plates of crawdads and some alligator strips, no frog legs."

"This is the second night you've treated us all to dinner," said Melissa. She set her elbows on the table and pointed at Archie. "So how much money do you really have?"

Josh looked at her in feigned shock. "Talk about indecency."

"What, shock from you moochers? You deadbeats probably never bring your wallets when Archie's around."

It was Archie's turn to hold up his hand for peace. "No, it's okay, really. It's not that complicated. I inherited the house and a lump of cash to take care of my everyday expenses, and the only caveat is that I spend a select amount on my friends, which was a stipulation in the will. There are a couple of medical patents that generate additional income, and a percentage of that I'm also required to spend on my friends which I do with great reluctance."

Josh pointed his finger back at Melissa. "See, he has to pay our way even though he doesn't really want to, it's in the will."

"Anyways," Archie continued, "good old Dad knew that the best way to insure that his kids didn't turn out to be stingy monsters was to compel them to share."

Melissa pointed back at Josh. "Maybe you can jettison these losers, and take us in their place."

"Fat chance," said Josh.

Melissa bristled at the fat connotation.

"Remember," continued Josh, "the will said 'friends', as in friendly."

"At any rate," said Archie, "the biggest beneficiaries of Dad's largesse tend to be the eating establishments in this quaint little town of ours. And the really good news is that there is an ample supply of funds to provide for a larger group of friends, should it become necessary."

"You like to use a lot of big words don't you?" said Harley.

The waiter brought the drinks and spread them around. Harley frowned at the waiter who had no undershirt and when he placed the pitcher in front of him did so with an armpit in his face. Harley quickly poured out a mug of beer and passed the pitcher to Archie. When they all had drinks in hand, and while most of them were already drinking from them, Marlena raised her glass and cleared her throat. "Ahh aahh hem."

Josh looked up from his gulping. "Oh right."

Marlena smiled and clinked her glass with Archie's. "Simply said, here's to friends."

"To friends," said Archie.

The others knew better than to grumble, and rose their glasses before drinking, but not one of them acknowledged with a word.

Archie tipped his glass at Angie. "So I heard you had a little scuffle at the airport today," trying to break the ice. And it worked, for a moment. Angie lit right up.

"Some big shot from DC was trying to gum up the works, wouldn't move his car, acting like a tough guy, flashed his badge at me and called me a bad name, so I let him have it."

"Let him have what?" asked Marlena.

Bob chimed in from the side. "I heard the report. Simultaneous taser and mace application." He tipped his glass towards her in appreciation. "Salud."

She shrugged. "The creep had it coming."

"So what's the decision, what'd they give you?"

"Administrative leave for two weeks while they do an investigation." She nodded at Marlena. "It's a standard thing whenever force is required. Lucky thing for me they found a fresh ounce of local grown marijuana on the good old Senator. He's got some splainin' to do."

"Nice," said Bob.

Angie smiled. "Daddy didn't raise no dummy."

The band was on the stage and tuning up. A funny looking trio, they were all dressed in hillbilly attire ranging from boots and overalls, to a flowered dress and floppy flowered hats. They tuned up rather quickly and with a one and a two they were off with some foot stomping music.

Marlena grabbed Archie's hand and dragged him to his feet and off to the dance floor. The music was actually quite good. The bass player was sitting on a stool thumping away on what looked like a broom handle stuck in an upside down metal can with some clothesline strings attached, the banjo was plucking away, while the violin filled in the gaps with a constant flowing river of sweet sounding notes.

Angie was smiling while she watched the

dancers and the band, and bouncing her hand on the table, while tapping her foot and it could be said that this was approaching true foot stomping music.

"Enjoying yourself?" asked Bob.

"Bite me," she replied.

"Alright," said Harley. "Here's the deal. We found out that Archie has tickets on the Thursday evening flight off the island."

"That's tomorrow," said Melissa.

"Yes Melissa, you win a prize, that is tomorrow. They have a connecting flight in L.A. and then fly non-stop to Paris arriving Friday night. They'll be there Saturday and Sunday, somewhere on the river Seine or some fancy old place where they eat frog legs and snails, and that's probably when he'll do the proposing that *we* propose to block."

Melissa set her glass down and gave her report. "She doesn't know where they're going. All Archie told her was to pack a suitcase for the weekend and to bring a passport."

"That bastard," said Josh.

"Archie's pretty wily," said Harley.

"I don't trust him as far as I can throw him," said Josh.

"Our job," continued Harley with a sidelong glance at Josh, "is to block him from picking up Marlena and getting to the airport." He held up his hand to stop Josh's side comments. "Your job girls, is to block Marlena from meeting up with Archie. Somehow we have to circumnavigate their movements on that day, cut off their communication. We'll make this such an ordeal, such a fiasco, that Marlena will see what a jerk Archie really is, and vow never to see him again." He pounded the table for effect.

Betty smirked; she'd been silent the whole night so far. "Ha ha, so this is your big plan Harley? You think she's going to vow never to see him again if they miss a little flight?"

Harley sat back in his chair. "Well…"

"You're living in a dream world. This whole Archie and Marlena thing is probably inevitable. I mean look at them on the dance floor, don't they look happy?"

"Ahh…"

"But just because they're a potential couple that may be inevitable, doesn't mean that this whole thing with all of us getting together all the time is inevitable. I mean is anyone here having fun?"

She looked around the table for answers and they all shook their heads or looked away. "We can get out of these little get togethers. But they may not. They could be on a path that keeps them together for a long time, and there's nothing that they, or us, or anyone else can do to stop it. We, and I mean us girls, think differently than you guys do. We just don't want our friend to rush headlong into anything, get all googly eyed in some exotic location and get cornered into something that she should really be taking a good look at before leaping. You know, like the old saying, look before you leap? That's what our plan is, not to 'break them up', but to delay this little trip for a while. So I guess in a sense we're on the same page."

The table was silent for a moment.

"All I heard was that we're on the same page," said Bob.

"Okay then," said Harley, "here's our part of the plan. Listen up people."

He looked around to make sure nobody nearby could hear, and just to make certain he started talking in a low voice while the rest of them leaned in to hear better. "I'll flatten Archie's tires before dawn, then Josh will swing back by and 'help' him fix the tires and strip a couple of lug nuts in the process, Archie will lose his temper, then call me for assistance, and I'll make sure the auto parts suppliers have to order the parts and it'll take half the day to get it from the other side of the island. Meanwhile Archie will be coming unglued, and we'll be there to 'help' him some more. Bob will stop by, and being the luggage expert that he is, help him pack his bags so he won't get pulled over by security in a foreign country, and in the process plant some contraband in the edges of his suitcase to make the trip more exciting."

Bob nodded. "C-4 explosive residue, we use it for training at the airport. He won't get very far."

"Meanwhile," Harley continued, "Josh will accidently break a pipe in the kitchen while getting a drink of water, flood the house, and while trying to stop the leak knock Archie's cell phone into a puddle, and short out the electric grid and landline for the entire house."

"I'm a klutz in the morning," said a grinning Josh.

"No one else will bring their phone to our little going away party," continued Harley, "and Archie won't be able to call Marlena to tell her that he's running late."

"Hey I've got an idea", said Betty, "why don't you just have someone in a runaway bulldozer smash Archie's car and ram through his house and completely destroy it?"

The guys tilted their heads as they imagined that scenario panning out.

Josh snapped his fingers. "I know a guy with dozer."

Harley shook his head. "Naw, too messy, let's keep this simple, but I like the way you're thinking Betty, total annihilation. Back to our plan. We'll convince Archie that we need to take a short cut on the old cane haul road over the center of the island to pick up the car parts, get stuck in the mud and after that we'll run out of gas, I'll forget to pack an extra gas can, and we'll have to hike out."

"The mud bog?" asked Bob.

"Exactly," said Harley, "mile marker five on the cane road, guaranteed always muddy even on drought months, plus that road is such a bitch to drive on, sorry girls, that no one ever uses it and we don't have to worry about anyone showing up to give us a ride. I'll forget to bring drinking water, which will further slow us down, and by the time we make it back to the highway to hitchhike home, it'll be late afternoon, and Archie'll be all worn out."

"Poor little tyke," said Josh, "he'll be ready for a nappy nap."

Harley was finished, and looked over at Betty. "Okay, so what do you got? What's your plan?"

"Gee Harley, after all that, it sounds like we won't need to do much of anything."

Harley was disappointed. "What? You really got nothing?"

"Well, since you really need to know...," Betty glanced around suspiciously just like Harley to make sure they weren't being watched by spies, and spoke in a much lower tone so they all had to lean even closer to hear what she was saying. When she was sure that the coast was clear she started whispering. "We were thinking of spiking her coffee with sleeping medicine, then when she was out cold, stuffing her in the trunk of a car and shipping it off on the morning barge to Oahu, where she'd wake up the next day with a splitting headache, no money, no phone and no idea where she was."

Josh was into the idea. "Excellent," he said.

Harley saw right through the charade and pushed away from the table. "Look, if you're not going to be serious about this…"

15.

THURSDAY

The day of reckoning.

Harley sat in his shop at dawn's early light, shuffling paperwork in the office and waiting by the phone for Archie to call for help with his car.

He'd gone over to Archie's house well before dawn, when the sky was still black as night, let the air out of three tires, and gave one of them an ice pick to the sidewall to prevent any refilling. It was a tough thing to do to a new tire but there was no getting around it. Now Archie'd have to change that tire with his spare in the trunk, and Josh would be right alongside helping him.

'Any minute now,' he thought. 'Ring a ding ding. Harley, help, you have to come over right away, my tires are flat and that damned Josh stripped some lug nuts, hurry..." Any minute now. He looked at the clock on the wall, it was seven o'clock, and his mechanics were showing up for their shifts, waving at him and heading to the bays to start working on the cars they had lined up. Seven o'clock, Archie should be calling any minute...any minute now... He walked to the door and looked at the gathering light towards the East and hummed a little tune. High clouds filled the sky, and it looked like rain was on the way. By all appearances it looked like a bad day to fly. A very bad day indeed.

Across the way on the other side of the industrial center he could see his arch rival in the auto repair business, Alfredo opening up for business. Steady eddy Alfredo, the guy was like a damn clock, in at dawn, out at dusk, day after day, weekends and holidays. The putz didn't play golf but he was a top notch mechanic and always seemed to have one of his cars in the finals at the drag races on the West Side. Harley gave a little nod to him and got nothing in return. Typical. 'Just wait pal', thought Harley, 'I'm gonna blow you off the line just like last time'.

Harley wondered, 'What car is he gonna run at the races next week?' and then he saw his old buddy Manini pull up in his big black truck. Alfredo guided the evil looking vehicle into one of the bays and pulled the sliding door down, glancing around suspiciously to see if anyone was watching.

'Super secret eh?' Something was going down.

'It's Manini's truck,' thought Harley, that's what he's going to race, they're adding some muscle to it. You guys think you can get something over on me huh? Fat chance.

Half an hour went by. He didn't want to leave the shop until Archie called, but he also didn't want to call over to his house sounding anxious, Archie might put the flat tire blame on him. That guy had the worst streak of blamerism in the world.

At seven thirty five AM the phone rang. It was Josh.

"I'm at Archie's house, shucks I got here a little late, my alarm didn't go off..."

"Yeah, yeah. So why are you tying up my phone line, I'm waiting for Archie to call for help with his tires. You helped him strip some lug nuts right…right?...”

“He's not here, the car's not here.”

“Dang it Josh!” He squeezed the handle of the phone as though it was Josh's neck, and the plastic cracked. Deep breath. Calm. Think fast. Archie must have fixed the tires himself. No stripped lug nuts. No need to call for help.

“Alright Josh, no worries, you stay right there in case he comes back, okay? Maybe he went to grab breakfast or something.”

“Then what do I do?”

“Just stick to him like tarpaper, get in his way, bumble around, break some things like we planned, the faucet for instance, or a door, something to piss him off. Let me know when he gets back, and I'll think of something else to slow him down.”

He hung up the phone and took another deep breath. Shouldn't have trusted Josh with the job. The plan was too damned convoluted anyways, stripping a lug nut turned out to be a lame idea; everything they planned hinged on that stupid move. He should've just done something simple like pulling the ignition coil or swiping the differential, something that would make the car totally inoperable with the part only available Oahu or the mainland. Archie was probably driving around the island now, all paranoid, thinking some crazed vandals let the air out of his tires, and not willing to let the car out of his sight again until he got on the plane and it was safe in the airport parking lot with security and cameras everywhere.

There was a deep rumble and a slow screeching of tires outside his office. “Now what?” he muttered. It was Manini, in the big black truck, right outside his door, turning the wheels in a tight circle, the new knobby tires squealing on the cement, completing the u-turn with the truck now facing back toward the road. He revved the engine, it sounded throaty and mean.

This can't be good thought Harley as he came out of his office and called out. "Can I help you with something?"

"Yeah," shouted Manini over the rumble.

"Yeah what?"

"Yeah, you can help me by standing right there so I can give you a little preview of what's gonna happen at the track next week."

Prisoner came trotting to the door and growled.

"Stay," warned Harley and the dog sat down next to his feet. "And hold your ears." Harley knew what was about to happen. He knelt down and covered Prisoner's ears with his hands. Manini jumped on the accelerator and the engine roared, tire tread melting smoking white and black rubber and the truck shot off down the driveway fishtailing as Manini fought for control. Prisoner broke away from Harley and bolted after the truck while barking his head off.

"No!," shouted Harley. "Prisoner!" But it was too late, the dog was on a mission to bite that damned black truck that was invading his territory. The Aussie Cattle Dog is one of the quickest dogs on the planet and if you saw that dog chasing the truck that was roaring full throttle down the driveway you'd believe it. Prisoner caught up to the truck as it reached the curve and *passed* it on the left. The truck nearly flipped over as the tires gripped the right hand corner going full speed and a chunk of knob separated from the tire and spit out backwards, hitting poor Prisoner in the hind leg with the force of a bullet from a gun. The little dog yelped and somersaulted into the air and tumbled into a ball of fur on the side in the dirt and lay still.

Harley and the mechanics were watching the melee of the truck barreling down the drive and when the dog tumbled to the side Harley yelled out and ran as fast he could towards him. When he got there Prisoner was whimpering and licking his back leg. Harley checked the wound as best he could without getting a bite for his trouble.

"It's just a flesh wound," he told the dog. "You got nicked, that's all, I've seen worse. C'mon, rub it off champ."

Prisoner stood up favoring the leg, then tested it out by limping around Harley wagging his tail and looking up for approval.

"You're not a good dog," Harley admonished him. "You're a bad dog, a very *very* bad dog. How many times have I told you not to chase cars? You disobeyed me, I told you to stay."

Prisoner's eyes went down and his ears tapered back, tail tucked between his leg, a guilty dog. He growled slightly at the departing truck that was heading over the hill in the distance. Trying to change the subject. Harley was about to scold him again when suddenly from the side of the driveway, hidden this whole time by a row of bushes, a bunch of kids ran over towards Prisoner, and he broke away from Harley to join them and they jumped around each other, Prisoner leaping in the air to lick their faces.

"We heard the race car and we came to watch Mister," said one of the kids, not more than five or six years old. "We're on our way to school." And suddenly Harley understood what just happened. Prisoner saw the kids on the side by the bushes and rushed out to save them. The truck was headed right for the kids who were watching from the bushes, and he put himself in harm's way, passing the truck on that side and using his little body as a shield. He couldn't have known that the truck was going to turn to the right on the corner. To the brave little dog, that bad man's truck was headed right for his friends and he had to save them, no matter what command Harley gave to him.

He reached down and ruffled Prisoner's fur coat and scratched behind his ears. "Good dog, good boy." And Prisoner just about came unglued, he was wagging his tail so hard it almost came off. "Some guys never learn their lesson do they? You're not supposed to race on the streets, you're supposed to save it for the track."

"You're not supposed to drive fast on the road," said one of the smallest boys. "That's what my Mommy says to my Daddy."

"Yeah," said Harley as watched the last of Manini's truck fade away over the hill, still gunning the engine. "Your Mommy's right, and I'm gonna fix that guys wagon, you just wait and see."

16.

They huddled up under the plumeria tree at the far end of the employee parking lot. From this vantage point they could see the entire airport from one end to the other.

Harley pulled out his binoculars and scanned the horizon to the east looking for the airliner. "Nothing yet, what time is it?"

Angie looked at her watch. "Six fifteen."

"Okay, twenty minutes until the interisland flight touches down, and then a twenty minute turnaround until it takes off again. That gives us forty minutes. It'll be dark in about ten minutes. Bob, check the tower communications."

"Roger," said Bob. He pulled out the scanner and adjusted the knob. They could hear the control tower radioing the different planes that were in the air, giving directions and double checking coordinates. They heard the words 'flight two five two' and some directions on altitude and turning.

"That's our guy," said Harley. "Alright people, we all know why we're here right?" They all nodded. "Stop that plane from taking off at all costs. We're blocking that trip to Paris. Are we all in?"

"Of course we're all in," said Betty, "we're here aren't we, standing right in front of you, c'mon enough already with the pep talk Sergeant."

"Sergeant Harley," he repeated, "I like that."

"Well don't get used to it."

Harley turned to Melissa. "Any sign of the Hummer yet?"

Melissa sighed. "Nope, I've been watching that entrance for so long my eyes are getting weary,"

"I had Archie's house staked out all day," said Josh. "He must have fixed his flat tires and never came back."

"Marlena left in a taxi early in the morning," said Angie. "I followed it to the mall but lost it in traffic, and I never could find her after that. She probably wanted to do some last minute shopping for the trip. I looked in all the usual stores."

"They're probably running late," said Harley.

"Hey, what if they're running so late they miss the flight?" said Josh.

Harley smiled. "Well that's all the better, miss their interisland flight, miss their connecting flight to the mainland, and miss the flight to Paris, perfect scenario, case closed. No proposal."

"Oh yeah," said Betty. "I forgot to tell you, we found out some inside info on Marlena, thought you might be interested."

"Yeah, what's that?"

"She's filthy rich. Her parents own some sort of mining operation in Brazil. Her bankroll makes Archie look like a beggar."

"Figures," said Harley. A hot rich ballet dancer from Rio. Falling backwards into money and pretty women, this time all rolled into one.

"Yeah," said Betty, "imagine that, all this time we thought she might not be getting such a bad deal with Archie and his money and all. But it turns out she'll be the one going down a few notches on the money ladder."

"The money ladder?" said Josh. "Is that what you girls call it?"

"Not all the time," said Melissa. "In your case we call it the loser ladder. Floor to ceiling, all loser, all the time."

"At any rate," said Betty, "Marlena doesn't want Archie to find out, just yet anyways. She kind of likes him thinking that she's on her own and independent, and completely able to support herself with her dance instruction."

"So why are you telling us?"

"Because we know how you guys think. Everything's a competition with you right?"

"She's got a point," admitted Bob from the side.

Harley stared at Betty and then nodded his head as he understood completely what was being said and why, and she saw that he knew.

"That's right," she said smiling, and pointed her finger at him. "Our friend has way more money than your friend, so we win."

Harley squinted his eyes at Betty in the dim light from the lamppost.

"All the more reason to keep them from getting married," he said. "That poor guy doesn't know what the heck he's getting into. He's been lied to from the get-go. He'll be double, triple henpecked with a woman who has more money than him, she'll be the one wearing the pants around the house, he won't know if he's coming or going, she'll be telling *him* what to do and when to do it, telling him to jump, and then *after* he jumps she'll tell him if it's high enough. Not only will there be no golf on a weekday for that sad sap, he can kiss weekends goodbye too. He'll be whipped morning noon and night for the rest of his miserable godforsaken life."

Betty smiled slyly. "See girls, just like I said. Male chauvinist pig through and through."

Harley shrugged his shoulders, picked up the binoculars and scanned the terminal building again. Randy was working baggage, Johnny boy was up front at the Agriculture inspection station and Boots was directing traffic. It was a busy night, and a lot of people were travelling right before Thanksgiving.

"Why in the heck do people want to travel around the holidays?" asked Harley. "Why don't people just stay close to home?"

"Have you ever thought they might want to visit their families who don't live with them?" asked Betty. She shook her head and whistled at the stupidity of his thinking.

"Oh yeah," Harley chuckled, "I guess you're right, never thought of it that way. Not everyone still lives with their families."

She knew that was a wisecrack about her, and her knuckles popped as she made a fist, while he kept scanning the terminal building.

"What if Archie parked somewhere else and caught a taxi with Marlena?" said Josh.

"Archie take a taxi?" Harley scoffed. "Not likely, he loves that silver Hummer. I'm surprised he isn't taking it along with them to Paris. He probably thought of it though. Oh no, he's gonna drive that vehicle to the very last second he can before he gets on that plane, which will NOT be taking off I can tell you that." He finished his scan of the terminal, and at the far right side was the taxi zone that served the direct mainland flights. He lingered the binoculars for a moment on the taxi zone. There was Stevie, shooting the breeze with another cabbie, sitting in his big white van waiting for some customers, he had a big TAXI painted in giant letters on the side of the van so no potential customers would miss him. A security agent in an orange vest was directing traffic as a long line of cars entered the terminal. He saw a flash of silver and chrome, and thought it was the Hummer coming down the road, only this one was in the parking lot at the very far end sitting there all by its lonesome...

"HOLY COW!" He jumped up knocking Betty to the ground, and zoomed in on the silver car. It was a Hummer. Archie's Hummer.

"What the hell is wrong with you?" Betty fumed as she got off the ground and dusted herself off.

"It's the Hummer, it's already here. Wait; let me check, maybe there's more than one like it on the island." He could see the little eyeball sticker on the windshield with the 'Here's looking at you' logo, stupidest damn car sticker on the island. "Nope, that's it." He slapped his knee. "They're already here. How the hell?"

"Well I've been watching that entrance for the past two hours," said Melissa. "They didn't come through there."

"There's no other way to get in the parking lot," said Angie. "They have to come in that one little entrance."

"They must have come early," said Josh. "That's why he never came home this morning."

"Archie get somewhere early?" said Harley. "That would just about be the first time for that guy, and it just had to happen today, of all days."

"So now what?" asked Betty.

"Plan B," said Harley. "Too late to have the cops grab them at the entrance, we'll have to roll out our contingency. Dang it, I didn't think we'd let them get this far. Bob, call in the bomb threat." Harley snapped his finger as he gave the order.

"Wasn't plan B the whole spreading 'innuendo'," mocked Betty.

"That was plan A. Plan B was flattening his tires."

"I thought that was plan T," said Josh.

"Alright, ALRIGHT! How about this is plan E for enough already!"

Bob just frowned and shook his head. "I'm not calling in a bomb threat to my own airport Harley. I don't know where you got the idea that I would do something like that unless it's totally, completely necessary."

"Okay then, go ahead and e-mail the fake terrorist alert report to airport security using our dummy phone, and attach those photos of Archie and Marlena. See if they can pull them on the side for some, 'questioning'. They're probably in the lounge, thinking they pulled a fast one on us."

"Now that I'll do," said Bob. Give those jackasses at security something to do."

He opened the smart phone and hacked into an online encrypted file dump site that he had set up earlier in the day and e-mailed the link of the photos to the airport security website. "That'll get their uniforms in a bunch. Can anyone say, 'strip search'?"

Harley turned to the others. "Josh, you and Betty go with Bob and Angie and Melissa, and run the contingency plan when that interisland flight lands. Let's make them all sweat a little down there on the tarmac during the turnaround." He pulled a small suitcase out of the back of the truck, opened it and checked the contents, a small cooler with ice bags, two stink bombs, a lighter, and a super soaker water pistol. Satisfied that it was all there, he handed the bag to Betty since she was the closest to him.

"Hey, what about you?" asked Betty as she took the bag.

"I've got a little surprise cooked up, a little diversion."

She looked at him with suspicion. "What kind of diversion?"

"Never mind, you'll know when it happens. If that plane gets to thinking about taking off again, believe me, it'll think twice."

"Planes don't think," said Josh.

Harley tried hard to keep his composure, speaking slowly. "Okay, if the pilot thinks about taking off, he will think more than twice when he sees my diversion." He took a little tin out of his pocket, dipped two fingers into it and started rubbing black goo on his face and arms, then put a floppy black hat on his head and backed into the shadows.

"Hey, that's pretty good," said Bob, "we can barely even see you, but if the guards on the perimeter see you looking like that, they'll probably shoot you. They have infrared night vision scopes you know."

They could see Harley's white smile in the darkness. "Way ahead of you Bobby, these clothes and black goo are infra red blockers. Those shmucks won't see a thing, now go on people, get going, do your good deeds, and I'll see you back here in twenty minutes. Mark your watches."

Bob looked around. "Anyone got a watch?"

They all shook their heads and held up empty hands.

"Oh well that takes care of that," said Bob. "None of us have watches Harley." There was no answer from the shadows. "Harley? Hey Harley!"

"He's gone," said Josh. "You know this whole scheme seems kind of sketchy all of a sudden. Maybe we should just bail out already, and go home."

"You know," said Bob. "That's probably the best idea you've had all day."

The three girls were standing on the side listening to the banter. All of them had their arms folded, and each one of them had a version of apathy on their faces.

"You guys are pathetic," said Angie.

"Worse than pathetic. Losers," said Melissa.

"Wimps," added Betty.

"You'd let your friend go out there with real danger on the line, maybe get shot or worse, and at the slightest sign of trouble, because you have no watch for heaven's sake, you'd ditch him."

"I think you two are cowards."

"Wusses."

"You see girls," said Angie. "This is another reason why we need to make sure that our friend doesn't get caught up in this little clique of theirs. Archie probably deep down has the same exact DNA as these clowns, and will leave Marlena behind if, and when the going gets tough."

Bob looked at Josh. "Did they just call us wusses?"

"You heard right," said Melissa.

"You know girls," said Betty, "When it comes

down to it, we really don't even need these guys for this job."

"Yeah, they'll probably just get in the way."

Bob was still looking at Josh. "No one calls us wusses, right Josh?" Josh just shrugged.

"C'mon girls, let's do this," said Betty, holding the black bag, and they all turned to walk away.

"You won't get very far without this." They stopped in their tracks and whirled around to look back. Bob was holding up a little white plastic card, dangling it in the air with his thumb and forefinger. "You got one of these? Do they hand these out to the meter maids, Angie?"

"Alright hand it over," she said.

"What is it?" asked Betty.

"This," said Bob as he inched towards them holding the card out tantalizingly close and waving it slowly, "is the key to the inner sanctum, you won't get on the field without this, will you Angie?"

She lunged for it and he held it high in the air while she repeatedly grabbed for it. Bob was laughing, and having a great time holding it just out of her reach while she jumped and jumped, till she kicked him in the shin and he dropped to the ground yelling in pain.

"Having fun Bob?" she asked sweetly.

"Alright, alright," he said, shielding his face just in case she went crazy on him. "We're going, we're going." He rubbed his shin in pain. "What are those, steel toed boots?"

They made their way across the parking lot, passing nonchalantly by the rental car booths, and lines of tourists waiting for the bus, and when the crosswalk light was green they walked across the entrance road and through an empty baggage claim area.

"This way," said Bob, and they headed for the far corner of the airport terminal, a dusty unused area at the northern end. Barbed wire fencing circled the field from here and all around the perimeter, and he led them to a little door at the edge of the building and the fencing. He looked back to make sure they were all still with him. The girls all had their hair pulled forward and covering their faces and he laughed out loud. "What the heck is this?"

Angie pointed to the camera above the door.

"It's out of order, been like that for about a year," said Bob, "that's why we're coming this way." He slid his card into the slot and then punched in a code and they heard a click as it unlocked. "Here goes nothing," he whispered and crossed himself before opening the door. It was a bare corridor brightly lit that led straight ahead, and he held the door open for them as they went through, and then peered out of it back towards the lobby and the road to make sure no one was watching them before closing it softly.

Being a highly trained professional in airport security, Bob shook his head as he looked at them lined up in the hallway with their backs against the wall like criminals in a police lineup. They were nervous.

"You guys look like you're up to something."

Angie scowled. "Well aren't we? What the hell Bob."

Josh was resigned to his fate. "We're all going to jail, aren't we." More like a statement of fact than a question.

"Look," said Bob, "you guys are with me, so relax, okay? I know this place like the back of my hand, remember that. This my domain, my inner sanctum, my coolio de condre, my…"

"Alright alright," seethed Angie, "we get it already, you own this place."

Bob acknowledged her with a wave of his hand. "Now you see, that's the kind of respect I was looking for. Just stick close to me, do what I say, and for the love of Pete folks, just relax. Look like you belong here, pretend you're on official business with me as your guide, get that thought and center it into your mind, make it your mantra, live it breath it feel it…"

"Shove it," said Betty. "We're wasting time. Get us down to the plane so we can do our dirty work and get out of here."

Bob instinctively cringed as the word bullwhip came suddenly into his mind and he looked quickly to make sure she wasn't actually carrying one hidden behind her back, maybe a small one for close work on an errant cow or human who got in her way.

"This way," he said with a frown and continued down the hallway. There was another door at the end, this one was unlocked and he opened it towards them and they entered a giant room, filled with machinery, tanks and valves and compressors whirring and hissing, blowers sending air through metal tubes running along the ceiling, while on the other side of the wall facing them was the sound of a jet engine whining to a stop.

"This is the air conditioning equipment for the entire airport!," yelled Bob over the noise.

"What?!" said Melissa, who was way out of her element. Bob just frowned at her and motioned with his thumb to follow.

They went through another door and the noise of the air condition units was replaced by the whine of jet engines, while a warm blast of jet fuel air and hot rubber hit them. Melissa held her nose. "God, that stinks."

"C'mon, let's go." Bob led them down a metal fire escape stairway to the tarmac. They were under the edge of the jet's wing, and they could see workers on the other side of the plane unloading baggage from the fuselage into a baggage cart. He pulled them over to an alcove where they could survey the scene in secret. "Alright it should take no longer than five minutes for them to unload the bags, and then we go to work, we'll have a five minute window before they start loading a new batch into the plane." He reached into the black bag he was carrying and pulled out hats and glasses, and overalls, and spread them around. "Quick, put these on."

Angie took one look and scoffed. "Those are sunglasses Bob. It's night time."

"You want to be in the newspapers tomorrow? Put 'em on!"

She grabbed a pair angrily from him. "You don't have to yell, jerk!"

"Stuff your hair up into the hats, make them wide like this first…" he reached over and tried to show Angie how to expand the hat, and they had a brief tug of war till she pulled it away from.

"I know how to do it…"

When the girls all had their hair stuffed into the hats and their sunglasses and overalls on, Bob slid his sunglasses onto the bridge of his nose and looked them over as though he were manning a uniform inspection in the military. He pointed directly at Angie and Betty.

"Straighten that out, button that up…"

"I'm getting ready to button something up alright," seethed Betty.

Bob knelt down on the asphalt and motioned them to get closer, and they circled around him. He got out a piece of chalk and drew a crude outline of an airplane on the blacktop and labeled the different areas with initials to indicate who went where. "Alright here's the plan, I didn't want to go over it until we were at the target area, so it'd be easier to see. Listen closely so I don't have to repeat myself. I downloaded the schematic of the plane but I forgot it at the car, so we'll just have to wing it." He pulled out two stink bombs and handed them to Angie. "Your job is to pop the tops off of these and get them into the air intake valves in the cargo section, here and here." He drew two 'x's' at the front of the plane. "It'll take a couple of minutes for the stink to get up into the cockpit." Then he pulled out a first aid instant ice pack and a roll of duct tape, and handed it to Betty. "You Bonzai, break this ice pack to get it going and tape it onto the thermostat in the belly of the plane. It's right on the side of the intercom next to the little elevator. The computer will think the inside of the plane is freezing and jack up the heater. You, Josh and Melissa take these screwdrivers," he handed them each a heavy tool. "And let the air out of the back tires. It'll trigger a warning light in the cabin. The valve is located above the tires in the strut, it looks just like a regular old tire valve on a car except it's not on the tire, it's halfway up the strut okay? And another thing, the air isn't regular air, it's nitrogen, so don't breath it or you'll get sick. You either gotta hold your breath, or turn your face away from it as you release it."

Melissa wasn't only claustrophobic, she had a hard time holding her breath and her face scrunched. "What? How long do we have to hold our breath?"

"I don't know, thirty seconds should do it."

Thirty seconds of not breathing. Thirty seconds of sheer panic. "I want to switch," she said and even saying that short sentence seemed to drain all the breath out of her. She reached out the screwdriver to Angie and grabbed for the icepack. "Here, you do the tires, I'll do the thermostat."

Angie shook her head and held the icepack behind her back. "No way girlfriend, you got the tires, just deal with it."

She reached out the screwdriver to Betty. "Can I switch with you, please?"

Betty just shook her head and scowled. "Girl, you're just making us look bad in front of these guys. Now just do it."

Melissa looked at Bob and he just shook his head. "No way."

Josh reached his hand out, "It's okay Melly, I'll do both the tires, you can wait over here in the shadows where it's safe."

He hadn't called her Melly in a long time, and in her current fearful state of mind, she nearly gave in to that fear. And then the most amazing thing happened. She gathered a spoonful of courage from the bottom of her soul and it spread throughout her entire being, and she stood straight and proud and stiffened her upper lip, and nearly shouted. "I've got this!"

Bob held up his hands for her to be quiet, and they all instinctively cowered at her yelling.

The whine of jet engines and baggage trucks racing to and fro were the only sounds that surrounded them as her yell dissipated quickly into the air.

Bob looked over to check on the baggage team's progress. They were almost finished, the guys who were standing on the ground by the luggage carts were taking off their gloves and stuffing them in their pockets, while their co-worker who was up in the cargo area jumped down to join them.

"Now listen," he continued looking directly at Angie. "You'll have a maximum of three minutes in the cargo pit before you gotta get out of there, understand? Three minutes to ice the thermostat and set off the stink bombs, and then jam."

"What are you gonna do?" asked Angie. "Stand over here and hide?"

Bob frowned. "Woman of no faith." He smiled as he pulled a large super soaker water gun out of the bag.

"Gonna play water tag?" mocked Angie.

"This isn't water," he said and squirted a tiny bit on the ground. "It's hydraulic fluid. This little squirt gun has been tested to thirty five feet of pinpoint accurate streaming spray, and it's gonna go right onto the windshield of that plane once you've all done your' jobs and are in the clear. The pilots will be going through their checklist for takeoff, and suddenly the cockpit will heat up, there'll be an unmistakable stink in the air, the tire pressure warning light will start flashing, and then when they see hydraulic fluid on the windshield they'll scrub the flight while we make our getaway."

"Sounds like you've thought about everything," said Betty while Bob nodded proudly.

"I have."

"Well what about that guy?" She pointed to a golf cart coming their way. It was being driven by a balding man dressed in blue security suit. He was stopping at each door along the way, getting out and checking it to make sure it was locked, then hopping back into the cart and going to the next. The section they were at had a row of doors, maybe twenty or so, spread out over a hundred yards, storage for the tarmac crew

"Damnit," whispered Bob, and they all pressed back along the wall into the shadows.

"Who is it?" pleaded Melissa.

"It's the boss. I don't know what he's doing here, he should have left hours ago." He looked quickly around, there was nowhere to hide, they were trapped like rats. He scuffed the chalk drawing of the airplane with his shoes and made a decision. "Here, quick," and he pulled them towards a door nearby, using his security card he punched in a code, hustled them in and closed the door behind them, and when he turned the light on briefly they were all blinded since their eyes were adjusted to the darkness outside, and he quickly turned it back off. Burned onto their retinas were quick images of the contents, stuffed into the storage closet were stacks of orange cones, blocks for the plane tires, cables and ropes and portable lights, and an overwhelming odor of rubber mixed with oil and dust.

"I think I'm going to be sick," said Melissa.

Bob tried to lock the door, and fumbled at the knob. Angie pulled out her phone and the dim glow showed them why he was having such a hard time locking it. There was no damn lock on the inside of the knob, probably so a numbskull couldn't accidently lock himself in, like the doorknobs on freezers in restaurants and stores.

They could hear the golf cart getting closer, and the security guy jiggling knobs. Now they were really trapped like rats.

Bob had his ear to the door. "Here he comes." He grabbed onto the doorknob and pulled hard against it and wedged his foot against the wall for leverage. The door opened outwards and if he could just hold it long enough, maybe the guy would think it was locked and go away.

The security guy was whistling as he got out of the cart in front of their door, and checked the knob twisting it over and over. "That's strange," he said. Even though the knob felt tight and wouldn't move, it didn't make the usual clicking sound when rotated against the metal locks in the knob. He tried harder, and Bob struggled to maintain a grip.

"My hands are too slippery," he whispered.

Angie reached over and grasped onto the tops of his hands, wrapping her small hands over his and squeezing tight.

Bob smiled a little. "Hey, that feels kinda…"

Before he could say the word 'good', Angie ground her heel into his free foot and he stifled a yell.

The security boss sighed and got out his card and slid it in the slot by the knob to unlock it and tried again. Still stuck. He leaned against the door with all his weight, jiggling the knob.

"What the hell is going on here!" He pulled out his microphone and clicked the switch. "Dispatch, this is Royce. Get some maintenance guys down here to check a door on the tarmac." He looked at the lettering. "Door number A-five-five. The damn lock is stuck, probably needs a shot of graphite powder to loosen it up."

"Roger that," crackled the response. "Be about twenty minutes though boss, we got a situation here in the main terminal, one of the baggage conveyor belts is stuck."

"Not a priority, just get 'em down here when they're free ." He gave the knob another twist and a curse for good measure and got back in the cart and moved onto the next door. In the room with ears against the door they could hear the electric cart noise fade away.

"We lost some precious time," whispered Bob. "But we're in luck, the baggage conveyor is stuck, so they're probably having a delay getting the next flight's bags to the plane."

"Can we just get the hell out of here?" pleaded Melissa.

"Well certainly," said Bob in a mock indignant tone. "I can't abide by all the cursing in here." He ever so slowly cracked the door open and first with one eye, and then the other peered out, then quickly popped his head out, looking towards where the golf cart was headed. It was gone. "Coast is clear, let's go."

They lined up again in the shadows next to the wall and Bob gave them a final briefing.

"Alright team, we have one shot at this, so let's make it count okay?"

"Roger that," said Josh and brought his hand to his brow in a salute.

Mellissa gave him an icy look.

"Why, isn't that airport lingo? I heard the other guy say it."

Bob looked towards Betty and Angie and they nodded.

"Let's do this," said Angie.

"Time to call in threat one," said Bob.

"What the heck does that mean?" asked Betty.

"Bomb threat," said Angie. Bob likes to talk in airport security lingo to make himself look big.

"No way," said Melissa. "That's a federal offense, you're going to get us all in big trouble."

"Aww, don't worry about it," said Bob. "We do these drills all the time. It's part of the job, we gotta be on our toes." He pulled out the throw away cell phone he'd picked up with cash from the megastore and dialed up the main security office. When a voice answered on the other end he spoke slowly in a deep voice while keeping his hand over the receiver.

"There is a bomb in a trash can at the north side of the terminal. I repeat, there is a bomb in a trash can on the north side of the terminal building." He wiped his prints off the phone smashed it under his heel and threw it in a trash can nearby. "That'll keep 'em busy for a while up there."

Another large airliner was landing on the far runway, tires skidding on the asphalt, the blast of the reverse thrusters pulling everyone's attention to the overwhelming sounds. There was nothing like being out on the tarmac at a busy airport at night. You couldn't really see them as they were dropping out of the sky and it sounded like the planes were landing right on top of your head.

The team fanned out to their areas, Josh and Melissa moseyed over to the landing gear, hiding next to the giant tires and began letting air out slowly, the hissing sounds imperceptible with all the other jet whining noise in the air. Betty and Angie waited for an opening and when the baggage trailer was far away from the plane they hopped up into the belly through the large cargo door. Bob watched as they disappeared up into the plane and he clicked his stop watch. He hid the plastic water gun under his jacket and headed towards the front of the plane. He could see the pilots in the bright cockpit flicking switches above their heads and talking to each other, and he took up a position next to a doorframe just under the nose of the plane with a good angle to the windshield and waited.

The luggage cars disappeared into the terminal and all was quiet around the plane. Everything was going smooth.

"I'm like the Godfather of this airport," whispered Bob as he smiled to himself. "No one gets in or out without my approval."

He saw Angie and Betty jump down from the cargo hold and join up with Josh and Melissa under the plane. The back tires were nearly half flat, and Bob's smile widened. All was going according to plan. He pulled out the super soaker, pumped it up and aimed it high over the cockpit window to adjust for wind, pulled the trigger and a steady stream of hydraulic fluid splashed all over the top of the plane and dripped down onto the windshield. 'Oh well," he whispered, "good enough,'. The pilots hadn't noticed the rose colored liquid on the glass yet, but they would.

"Hey you!" There was a loud shout from above and Bob winced as he looked up. It was the chief of security Royce, up on the catwalk above the roof.

"What the hell," hissed Bob, "doesn't that guy ever go home!" He slinked back into the shadow and he could see the chief talking into his radio. On the other side of the field flashing lights and sirens sprang to life as patrol cars raced towards the plane. He wiped his prints off the water pistol, tossed into a trash can and ran along the corridor in the shadows towards the exit door.

"Time to go guys, c'mon now." He slithered along the doorways while waving frantically at the others who were huddled around Melissa. Something was wrong.

Betty had the loudest voice and yelled out. "Her bracelet is stuck!"

"Break it!" he yelled back.

"It's her Grandmothers!" was the shouted reply.

Bob weighed the options. Stay here and get fired and go to jail. Leave and have them hunt him down, and then *still* get fired and go to jail. Either way, if those people under the plane insisted on saving Grandmas bracelet he was going to get fired and go to jail. Two other cars that were patrolling way down the field joined the first two in racing towards the airplane. To make matters worse he could see a handful of white shirted security men pour out of the terminal building nearby, pointing and yelling at the idiots under the plane. This was not looking good.

Bob thought fast and his eyes latched onto a big and beautiful yellow truck nearby. His eyes twinkled with happiness.

Normally the fire rescue trucks were parked in a hanger away from the terminal building and closer to the reef runway, but today they had a special event where they invited the local schools to see the trucks up close and personal, and even let some of the kids sit up in the driver's seat.

One of the trucks was still there. It was the big yellow tanker, the foam spreader, used when a plane lost its landing gear, and needed to do a belly flop.

He ran to it and jumped up into the driver's seat. The key was in the ignition, ready to rock and roll, and he fired up the engine and jammed it in drive, slammed on the gas pedal and it surged forward.

He yelled like a madman. "HAA HAAA HAAA!!!!!" . If he was going to go to jail he might as well make it worthwhile. He floored it full speed around the back of the plane towards the security guys that were running on foot and as he passed the plane he yelled out the window, "Break the damn bracelet!" It was dark in the cockpit but the lever marked FOAM was lit in orange and he pulled it. In the side mirror he could see the foam jetting from the back of the tanker. 'Now *that's* a super soaker,' he thought. The spray was jetting twenty feet from the side of the tanker and it covered the tail of the plane as he went by rolling up and onto the idiots as he lovingly referred to them now. Next up were the security guys running and when they saw the truck barreling right at them, foam jetting from the sides, they turned and ran for their lives.

"You'll never take me alive Copper!" he shouted with glee. He'd always wanted to shout that in a situation like this. "Not today Steve," he whispered as he foamed one of his buddies who was tripping and falling as he tried to escape the foam. "Take my sandwich from the break room fridge will you..."

The foam was going EVERYWHERE. He circled around the plane again and could see that his friends were now trapped in an island of calm in the midst of a foamy sea, the pilots and stewardesses were looking down from the windows at him in shock. The patrol cars were next and he chased them down and foamed them till they disappeared. He shut off the foam lever, pulled up next to the plane and stopped, and shouted towards the landing gear. "Get in, hurry!"

"We saved Grandma's bracelet," said Josh as they squeezed into the passenger seat onto each other. "It was stuck on a bolt, but the foam made it slippery and it came off."

"Why that's just fantastic," said Bob. "I couldn't be happier." More patrols were heading towards the scene, dozens of police cars, sirens and flashing lights ringing the airport, zeroing in on them. "Hey I've got an idea, how about we get out of here?"

"Why don't we just give up," said Angie. "Maybe they'll let us off with a warning."

Bob shook his head. "If we give up, you'll never get to be a cop. Me and Josh will never get to play golf again. Betty won't get to win the rodeo, and Melissa won't ever get to..." he turned to her, "what is it that you want to do if we ever get out of here?"

She shrugged her shoulders. "Well I guess I'd kinda like to *not* go to jail."

Bob nodded. "Fair enough then, let's all not go to jail and get the hell out of here."

"With a foam truck?" said Angie. "Don't you think we'll be kind of easy to track Bob?"

"Woman of little faith, I have a plan."

"If it's anything like your last plan we're in big trouble."

"We're already in big trouble. Just relax and enjoy the ride. We've come this far kids, a little more destruction won't matter much on our rap sheet now will it?" He smiled at them. "Trust me."

The foam ringing the plane was as high as the truck and he eased into it with the windshield wipers on full which didn't seem to help one bit. They couldn't see a foot in front of them in the sea of white save for flashing lights reflecting throughout the foam. Suddenly they came out into the clear.

They were surrounded, cops on the left of them, cops on the right. But there was a clear path straight ahead towards the storage area of the terminal building. Bob did some quick calculations. The truck cab was eight feet wide, ten feet high, the double wide storage doors... eight feet wide, ten feet high.

"Hold on," he said. "And duck in case there's shooting." He gunned the engine.

"Shooting? Damnit Bob, stop this truck right this instant!" shouted Angie, and when she saw everyone else ducking below the windshield line she quickly did the same.

Bob reached up and put the truck in drive and floored it, the truck rumbling towards the terminal. He pulled the foam lever again for good measure as he ducked. Shots rang out and the front and side windshields shattered, glass raining down on them as the truck barreled forward. They all yelled and screamed as the truck barreled forward then crashed through the double doors and suddenly and violently stopped, wedged into the opening, the back of the foam truck tight on the brick and mortar opening, while the front of the cab was inside the storage area, the back of the truck was still bucking as the tires ground forward but couldn't move the truck any further into the opening. Bob put it in park and turned off the engine.

"Alright everyone out!" he yelled as he kicked out the remaining glass from the front windshield, crawled over the steering wheel and reached his hand back to help the others. The headlights of the truck were still on and they could see they were in a large, mostly empty storage room filled with swirling dust from their crashing entrance. The truck was completely wedged into the opening and not a crack of light from the outside was visible but they could hear the commotion from the frustrated police and security banging on the truck and yelling and chipping away at the bricks with crowbars and axes. Trapped like rats again. They stood at the front of the truck in the beams of light covered in foam and dirt and not a few angry faces.

"Great, now what genius?" fumed Angie.

He was about to say 'Woman of no faith' again but had a feeling it might get him slapped by an angry mob of women and one Josh.

"Remember when I said I know this airport like the back of my hand? Well I wasn't kidding. Step this way." He pushed aside boxes and crates and brought them to the wall at the back of the storage room. There, attached to the wall was a metal rung ladder that led to a trap door on the ceiling. "Fire escape ladder that leads from the air-conditioning room to the tarmac. Not many people know this, but these storage rooms were added on after the airport was originally built and there's a couple of these escape ladders that used to lead right onto the ground floor...."

Angie yelled. "Go!"

He quickly climbed the ladder and pushed through the trap door. 'Thank God no one locked it from above,' he thought. They scampered after him through the opening and were now huddled in the back of the machine room, the steady whir and hiss of the compressors blocking out the sounds of the sirens below. Bob looked at them in the bright lighting from the ceiling. They were a mess, covered in dust and foam and glass. "We'll stick out like a sore thumb," he mumbled. "Let's dust off a little shall we...maybe we can try to blend in a little, it'll be dark outside..."

The girls shook their heads. "Guys are funny," said Angie, and unzipped her blue crew suit and stepped out of it looking bright and cheery in clean clothes.

He'd forgotten they were wearing the coveralls. "I knew that," he said as he and Josh followed suit. Within seconds all the overalls were in a heap on the floor and they were headed to the corridor and safety. They walked out from the behind the machinery through the metal door and into the corridor leading towards the perimeter. It was empty. A miracle. They scooted down the corridor expecting to be handcuffed at any moment, and huddled at the exit door. It was so quiet and peaceful in the corridor, almost like a museum.

"Everybody just act normal," said Bob, cringing as he turned the handle and looked out the door and saw that it was a madhouse outside.

Cops and security were swarming all over the

place, sirens wailing, tourists running for cover. It was a crazy scene. He closed the door again relishing in the quiet, and turned to them again. "Let's go."

They slithered out through the crack in the door and were quickly on the outside. The parking lot was just across the entrance road that was right in front of them and just a stone's throw away. So close they could almost touch it, and they started walking forward, whistling and humming and looking around in awe like they were hillbilly tourists on vacation and had never seen an airport before.

A white shirted security guard came hustling around the corner, black shoes skittering on the concrete, keys and mace and taser clinking on his belt, running full speed next to the side of the building towards them. His face was grim. They stopped walking and huddled together again for safety. They're busted, of that much they are convinced, to a man and to a woman they know that the jig is finally up, it's the end of the road, and their shoulders slump as they group together, shoulders touching, ready to be herded into the paddy wagon never to be seen or heard from again.

The security guard knows them, it's Randy from baggage inspection, and he skittered to a stop in front of them, his was face red and sweating, wild darting eyes, voice high pitched with excitement and adrenalin. "Hey Bob and Angie, what are you guys doing here?"

And suddenly Bob knows they've been spared.

Bob tries to speak but his voice is mired in quicksand. "Oh nothing really," struggling to make his mouth move, "uh... we just came down to see some friends off, yeah that's it… they're heading off to Europe for a vacation, and uh, we actually just got here, imagine that. What the heck's going on Randy?"

"What's going on? What's going on! What's *not* going on is more like it. All hells breaking loose Bob. There's a bomb threat, someone sabotaged flight seven-oh-five, they stole a fire truck, unloaded all the foam on the tarmac and crashed it into the terminal. We think we got 'em cornered down there in the one of the storage rooms. I gotta lock off this door pronto, we're shutting down the whole airport. It's the most action we've ever seen man. In fact you guys better get the heck out of here unless you want to be stuck here for the rest of the night. I heard they're calling in a SWAT team from Oahu. This is big-time, big time I tell you!"

It's at that moment that Bob notices a small chunk of tarmac foam that had gone undetected and was sitting right on top of Angie's shoulder and he quickly put his arm around her while placing his hand on the offending object.

Randy's eyes squinted and gave them an all-knowing look as he said, "Back together again huh? I knew it would happen. Now scoot, unless you want to clock in and get to work."

"Yeah, well." said Bob looking around at his co-conspirators whose faces were sheet white, mouths open, still frozen with fear and anxiety. "What do you say peeps, shall we hustle on out of here and let this fine security agent get to work and find the bad guys?"

He didn't have to ask twice. They shuffled forward like a herd of sheep while Randy ran to the door, threw the bolt across the front of it and radioed in his position.

Fire engines, police, SWAT helicopters and the works descended on the little airport. They scuttled across the entry road, dodging police and fire trucks and made their way back to their plumeria tree at the back of the parking lot.

The airport was swarming with action as though someone had shaken up a hornets nets, people were being ordered to the ground and hustled out in squad cars, guns everywhere.

Out of the controlled turmoil a thunderclap sent everyone to the ground as a huge explosion rocked the far end of the runway, and a fireball erupted into the night sky, the flames roiling and twisting upwards. The shockwave across the parking lot triggered dozens of car alarms, and everyone within a mile looked up towards the sky with fear and anguish.

"What the heck was that?" shouted Josh from under a car.

"Harley…" Betty whispered, and they all looked in silence at the ball of fire that still steadily rose into the sky.

"Whoa," said Josh. "Look at the size of that thing…"

The police and firefighters all stopped what they were doing, their faces lit with the glow as they stared in awe at the sky and suddenly one then more jumped into their vehicles and raced off in the direction of the blast.

No one under the plumeria tree was the least bit amused by this turn of events. The night had taken a somber and perhaps deadly conclusion.

"He said he was going to make a diversion, said

Bob. "I hope he didn't blow his dang self up." The minute he said it, he wished he hadn't.

Betty wiped away a tear that had somehow formed in the corner of one of her eyes. "Idiot," she whispered.

They waited and watched as the fireball died out until all that remained was a dull glow on the edge of the night. Seconds dragged into minutes.

A hoarse and ragged voice from behind them bellowed as though from a bullhorn. "Hey, what are you guys doing?"

They all cringed with fear, for by the sound of the angry and gruff voice it just had to be the cops, security, the FBI, CIA, *and* the NSA all rolled into one. They were all going to jail for the rest of their lives, and they turned slowly to see Harley, his shirt torn to shreds, covered in ash and soot, hair and eyebrows singed off, the edges of his clothes still smoking. Betty rushed over and threw her arms around him and crushed him with a bear hug.

"Idiot," she whispered in his ear.

"Hey, hey hey," he soothed. "I told you guys I was going to make a diversion. And that was one heck of a diversion." A pack of police cars whizzed by heading towards the orange glow. "Check it out; they're all heading that way, the coast is clear, let's get out of here." He stood there in his smoking shirt with his palms up. "C'mon guys, what are we waiting for?"

"What the heck was that Harley?" asked Josh.

"Oh you know, a little bit of this, a little bit of that. Mostly C-4 and gasoline. Put it all in Manini's new truck, parked it out past the runway in a ditch, lit the fuse and KABAAM! The fuse was a little too short though…my demolition skills are a little rusty…"

He wiped his hand across the top of his head and came away with hair and burnt scalp, and then shrugged and smiled as the girls squealed. "Oh well, I say it was worth it. That's one plane that aint gonna make the connection. They'll probably shut down this whole airport until tomorrow. End of story, the trip to Paris is blocked my friends."

All of their cell phones started ringing at once and they pulled them out of their pockets.

"Text message," said Josh.

"From Archie," said Bob.

"From Marlena," said the girls in unison.

Josh read his first. "Check this out; it says 'Hey guys, we decided to take the early morning flight. I figured the airport would be a little crazy tonight if you know what I mean, plus I thought you guys might still try to talk me out of it or something. Ha-ha. Better luck next time. I'll see you this Sunday at noon for our game.'" Josh closed the phone. "Holy cow, he knew what we had planned."

"Dear girls," read Betty. "Looking forward to a fun time in Paris, wish you were all coming along. Sorry I missed you this morning, but Archie thought it was best to leave on the early flight. See you on Sunday. By the way I'm thinking about taking up golf. OMG - XOXO – Marlena."

"Thinking about taking up golf," sighed Angie.

"Going over to the dark side," said Melissa shaking her head in despair.

"You know girls," said Betty wistfully. "I've been thinking about doing the same thing…"

"Going over to the dark side?" asked Melissa.

"No of course not. Golf, I'm thinking about

taking up the game. I played when I was a kid, and I remember having a blast at it. I mean, why let these knuckleheads have all the fun?"

Harley almost couldn't believe the words he was hearing and he looked at her with new found respect and somehow muscled up the courage to ask her a question that he'd wanted to ask for long time. "Hey Betty, would you want to um…you know, go get a burger or something?"

He tried to be a slick guy and smooth the top of his head but only came away with more burnt hair sticking to the palm of his hand. "Well, maybe some takeout food?"

The usual 'Get Lost Loser' reply that she always had ready, lingered on her lips for a moment and then she hesitated and softened. "Alright, I'd like that Harley." She turned to her friends and shrugged her shoulders. "What do you think girls; maybe we should all go out together?" She motioned her head towards the other guys standing on the side looking like lost puppies without a hope in the world.

Angie and Melissa slowly turned towards Josh and Bob, and the four of them eyed each other sideways with fear and suspicion, and then all of the nonsense between them faded away into the night, and they smiled a bit at each other, and the smiles turned to gentle laughter as they relegated themselves to the inevitable, and began squeezing into the back seat of the car with Harley at the wheel and Betty sitting next to him, the two of them all alone in the front.

He looked at her with a serious glint in his eye, there was a question he needed to ask, before they moved any farther with their relationship.

"Were you really serious about playing golf again?"

Betty gazed deep into his eyes quietly for a moment, all thoughts of bullwhips and rodeos replaced by long fairways and bunkers and greens, and then she winked at him. "Absolutely. Match play, quarter a hole."

And for the first time in a very, very long time, Harley smiled.

www.ingramcontent.com/pod-product-compliance
Lightning Source LLC
Chambersburg PA
CBHW072223170626
46813CB00003B/1067